RIVETINGLY GREAT STORIES VOLUME 3

CONNOR WHITELEY

DEDICATION
Thank you to all my readers without you I couldn't do what I love.

INTRODUCTION

Back when I started writing, I thought I would only ever be able to write fantasy and science fiction books. Thankfully, that isn't true in the slightest because I happily write mystery and romance as well these days and I love all the four main genres.

However, I cannot deny that science fiction and fantasy are my "home" genres and these are the genres of fiction I keep coming back to time after time. I think them comforting, relaxing and they are so much fun to write. This is simply down to my writer and reader tastes because I love romance and mystery too, but science fiction and fantasy are my first loves in fiction.

It's why I love my *Agents of The Emperor* series. I created that entire fictional universe out of love for the genre and I wanted a space where I could write a whole bunch of standalone novellas with them being linked by the universe. It meant I could just keep writing, exploring and enjoy the science fiction world I was creating

My love for fantasy was why I created my *Fireheart Fantasy Series, my City of Assassins Urban Fantasy* series and now my Realm-related books that include *The Aleshia O'Kin Fantasy Adventure Trilogy, Rising Realm Epic Fantasy Series* and *The Cato Fantasy Series.*

It is my passion and interest in the genres that keeps me creating stories I have a lot of fun writing.

That's why I just had to combine the two when I was creating ideas for the 5 volumes.

And originally, you wouldn't imagine fantasy elements in science fiction stories would work, but they do because fantasy elements can be small or big, critical or less so to the plot of the story and high fantasy and space opera work really well too.

In addition, one reason why I was so passionate about creating a science fiction fantasy volume was because it would finally give me the excuse and motivation to start my Way of The Odessey Science Fiction Fantasy series. The idea for this series has been knocking about in my head for years now and it has been so nice to finally start the series.

You'll get to see what I mean later in the volume about this series being fascinating, rich and draws on a lot of fantasy and science fiction concepts. Yet it is so much fun too.

However, there are other short stories separate from that series too. For example, superhero psychologist Matilda Plum makes a few appearances in these pages as she deals with aliens and a whole host of other problems in an effort to help her clients.

If you know what psychology is actually about (and no it isn't profiling, mind control or any of that stupidity) then you'll find extra comedy in these stories as it is me basically taking the mic out of the myths and misconceptions about psychologists. I wish I had some of her superpowers but that isn't how psychology works.

Those are brilliant stories whether you're familiar with psychology or not.

Overall, there are a lot of fun, gripping, spellbinding stories in these pages so please enjoy, turn over the page and start reading some great magical stories set in the near and far future.

WET ALIEN

In all my life I had never ever thought too much about what a wet alien might smell like, have you? I might have imagined a wet alien to smell like wet dog, a wet snake or some kind of fishy thing, if I had dared to give the weird subject much thought which I seriously hadn't. I might have been a sex therapist to a past alien, I might have saved people from an alien terrorist, but what a wet alien smelt like?

Never.

I was sitting in my favourite place in the entire world, my therapy office, with its stunning bright walls that I had freshly painted, I managed to add a brilliant new egg chair to my growing collection of all different types of chairs to my office (not a psychological trick I promise) and my large brown desk had been freshly waxed by a very, very sexy superhero friend of mine. I had no problem watching his bubble butt as he waxed my desk.

Yet when the small furry, ball-like alien just appeared in my office I knew I was in for a hell of a day, and coming from me that had to be saying something.

You see my name is Matilda Plum, a superhero in the psychology, counselling and therapy sector of the world. Normally I help solve problems, treat their mental health conditions and I even save aliens on occasion but this was brand-new to me.

And it was the smell that really sent me over the edge into how weird this case was going to be.

The small furry alien smelt like peaches, watermelon and

coconut. It was one of the most overwhelming smells I had ever smelt before, it smelt like the alien had forced an entire ripe coconut into my nose and superglued it there.

At least I could enjoy the sweet tastes of the Caribbean on my tongue for ages, and if I get a bucket of sand and a hot man or woman serving me drinks then it would be like I was on holiday, all without the nightmare of air travel (even though I could just teleport there).

I actually might do that with my friends later.

As much as I loved the smell I sadly knew the scent of coconut, peaches and watermelon were going to cement themselves to my fabric chairs for months. I didn't mind it honestly, but what about my clients?

The entire point of my office was to create a heaven for them. And if they hated the smell of it then I might not be able to help tons of innocent people with mental difficulties.

This just wasn't on.

"Excuse me," I said to the small furry alien that didn't seem to have any eyes, ears or mouth. "I don't want to be rude but is there any way you could, you know, smell a bit less strong?"

The alien hopped up and down at me. I wasn't sure what he was saying but I felt the entire office collapse below me.

The next moment I was sitting in a large red leather chair at a brown conference table in some damp smelly cave. This smell was so much worse than the alien, it smelt damp, mould and the hints of rotten fish were simply awful.

I had no idea what was going on as no one else was sitting at the table so I used my superpowers to see where I was.

Granted in normal times, my superpowers come from all the myths and misconceptions surrounding psychologists, but given how there was no myth about psychologists having a built-in GPS, I should have to get creative.

Thankfully my superpowers didn't mind my creative licensing, because I knew I wasn't in Canterbury, England where I worked, lived and had fun with my friends.

I was actually in the Lake District hundreds of miles away, currently underground and there were tons of aliens about.

A flash of light next to me made me grin as I saw the most beautiful woman I had ever seen appear next to me. My boss Natalia, Goddess of Counselling, Therapy and Psychology, was wearing her normal stunning golden dress, long blond hair and she emitted a great golden light.

Then a minute later my two best friends Jack and Aiden arrived holding hands and looking a little flushed, as if they were having some adult fun when the alien appeared.

It was their day off from the practice so I couldn't blame them.

"Let me guess. Small like furry ball-like alien?" I asked.

Natalia grinned as did Jack and Aiden. Basically we had all been kidnapped by the same alien and that both excited and worried the hell out of me.

A moment later a large chunk of grey rock moved to one side like a sliding door and a very large muscular green-skin creature walked through. It was a walking fish with large biceps and six spider-like legs.

Natalia stood up like she knew this guy. "Most honourable Mouthpiece for the Lord of Tunnels, it is an honour to see you once more. If you had officially requested our presence, I am sure we could have bought you gifts of coffee, chocolate and squirmy cream,"

I just looked at Jack and Aiden. They were history buffs of our little team and if anyone knew who this alien was and why Natalia knew them, it would be them.

They looked as lost as I did.

Then the walking fish made a laughing sound and dissolved away like he was made from water.

"This is bad folks," Natalia said as she sat back down. "The Lord of Tunnels has kidnapped us and he is a very nasty alien that the Gods imprisoned here over three thousand years ago,"

I leant closer to Natalia, enjoying the scent of her perfume, and I bit my lip.

"Why would he kidnap us?" I asked.

Natalia shrugged. "I don't know but we called him the Lord of Tunnels because he is deadly, dangerous and he loves the darkness of tunnels. We need to get out of here now,"

I tried to teleport away but I couldn't and I could see in everyone's eyes that they couldn't either.

"Sorry about that Matilda Plum," a deep booming voice said.

We all looked at the speaker of the voice who was a very large humanoid creature with spider-like legs and blue scaly skin. He looked friendly but after years of experience in mental health I know how nothing is what it seems.

"Honourable Lord," Natalia said without bowing. "Why have you kidnapped us?"

The Lord grinned. "You have something I want and I need your help to save the lives of my species,"

I looked around at the smooth grey rock making up the cave and there wasn't a dent, a fault or anything that suggested another way out of here. And as much as I wanted to teleport away, because I now had the weird sense that we could with the Lord being here, all my superpowers were telling me this creature was in deep, deep trouble.

Maybe this Lord man was so arrogant he believed we wouldn't try to run away if he was with us. Sadly that idea was actually working.

I stood and Natalia reached for my wrist but I avoided her touch.

"What's the problem? And give me one good reason why we shouldn't teleport out of here right now?" I asked.

The Lord sat down in a large red leather chair that looked like it was about to break. "I kidnapped you here so I can kidnap you again and again until you help me,"

I nodded and sat back down as the little furry alien appeared again.

"There is a group of ten aliens in a nearby cave and they have stolen my coffee supply. The coffee supply is a holy relic to my species and without it, we cannot perform the needed rituals to continue the proud history of my species," he said.

I looked at Natalia.

"Virga," she said.

I went to laugh but seriously forced myself not to. I wanted us to escape here, not die.

"So you want us to retrieve your sex drugs?" Jack asked.

I busted out laughing and Natalia just smiled. The Lord of Tunnels looked furious but after a moment he smiled just a little.

"Yes, coffee is needed for my race. It is what makes us horny and kickstarts the biological processes in my species. Without it, we will all die in a few weeks,"

I nodded. That really did surprise me, I knew that all creatures lived for different lengths of time but only a few weeks, that seemed a little short. Especially for an alien that Natalia said she had imprisoned over three thousand years ago.

I stood up and Aiden and Jack came over to me. We sort of blocked Natalia from our conversation for some reason.

"The job is simple then?" I asked. "We just get some coffee back from some aliens,"

"Remember though," Jack said, "why did these aliens steal the coffee in the first place? If the theft of coffee is a matter of life and death then that makes them very dangerous,"

I smiled and we all nodded at each other. We did enjoy dangerous missions and venturing into alien territory certainly fit that bill.

When I turned around I gasped as I saw Natalia was hissing in pain as the little furry alien was sitting on her head and some of its foul hair was going into her ears and nose.

"If you fail me then I will kill your Goddess," the Lord of Tunnels said.

I went to step forward and maybe punch him but Natalia shot

me a warning look.

The Lord stepped towards me and he licked his lips. "And if you dare think of attacking me then I will take out my knife, flay you alive and fry up your crisp skin whilst you are still alive,"

I gulped.

"Then I will gut you, make you watch as your friends suffer the same and then as more and more Gods and superheroes attack to save you. I will do the same to them,"

I wanted to so badly kill him there and then but I was a superhero of psychology, I wasn't a fighter.

And even though I could normally read minds like nobody's business, I couldn't read an alien's mind very well. I had no idea what this guy wanted or intended to do.

"Enjoy," the Lord said as he tapped two spider legs on the floor and I felt the ground collapse below us.

Two seconds later we were surrounded by ten wooden aliens that looked like humans pointing spears at us.

It looked like we were in another cave area with smooth grey walls that were domed perfectly, a little stream cut through the rock and the scent of freshly roasted coffee filled the air. And I so badly wanted a refreshing latte at the moment.

"These peeps are okay," the aliens said as one as they pointed behind us.

I couldn't understand what the aliens wanted us to do until I turned around and noticed there was a large fire there that didn't give out any heat or sound. It was weird but I did enjoy watching the flames swirl, twirl and whirl around each other.

The bright flames seemed to be almost dancing with each other and having fun at the same time.

Me and Jack and Aiden went over to the fire and the wooden aliens joined us. They all sat around the fire like it wouldn't hurt them at all, in all honesty it probably wouldn't and come to think of it, I couldn't see the coffee at all.

I could smell it and it smelt amazing but I couldn't see any bundles of coffee, chocolate or cream. All the wooden aliens looked at us until the fire morphed into a bright red wooden alien with small pieces of fire dancing over his skin without hurting him.

I was seeing a lot of weird things today. I was so going to see that trip to the Caribbean later.

"Welcome Matilda Plum and her two sidekicks. Out of all the superheroes we hoped it would be you because you are the best," the fiery alien said, he had to be the leader.

I nodded but didn't dare speak. I wanted him to tell me everything first.

"I am sorry to hear about Lady Natalia, she was a good, kind woman when I last saw her and it is a shame the foul Lord has trapped her,"

"Give us the coffee and you can save her," Aiden said.

The ten wooden aliens pointed their spears at Aiden but the leader waved his fiery hand and they lowered them.

"What is so important about the coffee supplies?" I asked. "Can't you just go and get more?"

"When the gods imprisoned us down here they gave us ten coffee and chocolate plants and cows and the knowledge to turn these ingredients into what we needed," the leader said.

"But you killed them all," I said.

I had studied human civilisations enough to know the patterns they went through and I doubted these aliens were any different at the end of the day. Life always found a way to destroy itself.

"At first," the leader said, "we created a system where everyone owned nothing and the plants and cows belonged to the community. Then the Lord hated the system and he fought us to own all the plants for himself,"

"There was a fight and the plants were destroyed," Jack said.

"Exactly young superhero," the leader said. "Two plants remained and one cow. In the next hundred years the cow died and the plants were diseased,"

I stood up and paced around listening to the running of the

stream as I realised that my superpowers were trying to tell me something here.

I could partially read the alien's mind or at least his emotions and he was lying to me. I didn't doubt that the events described happened, I just didn't believe they happened in that order.

The smell of watermelon appeared around me and I felt like Natalia was trying to reach me but the damn furry bastard was stopping her.

Then I realised that these aliens were imprisoned down here by the Gods. They weren't always perfect but they always, always had their reasons and I never argued with their reasoning. It was sound.

I looked at Jack and Aiden and gestured them to come over to me.

The wooden aliens stood up with their spears and looked like they were about to attack us.

I didn't dare put my back to them but I had to see what my best friends thought.

"The gods imprisoned them for a reason and it had to be bad. The gods don't put good and bad people in the same place," I said.

"I think I know the reason," Aiden said looking at his boyfriend.

Jack bit his lip and nodded. "Three thousand years ago there was an attack on the Gods by strange creatures from inside the Earth. The creatures invaded trying to kill off the Gods and superheroes,"

I felt a pointy spear jab me in the back.

I jumped. I didn't know how the aliens had gotten behind me but they had us surrounded.

"The plan is simple really," the leader said. "This is where the species ends. Our species with all our different looks, accents and powers will end shortly,"

I nodded as I finally understood what was happening here. There was a reason why this species was imprisoned, why it was *still* imprisoned three thousand years later and why the Gods didn't talk about it.

I might not have been as much of a history buff as my best

friends but I knew how the Gods operated and there was always method to their madness. And these aliens were proof of that, the Gods wanted to test on them.

The gods wanted to see how these aliens would function if left to their own devices without being able to invade the surface, kill the surface dwellers and attack the Gods.

Clearly the gods realised that the aliens weren't friendly and they were all about killing, hurting and using violence against others. So the gods probably wanted to see if they could change that by themselves, but they couldn't.

The Lord of Tunnels was probably a title passed down through the generations that Natalia recognised for the trick it was, and maybe Natalia had realised that the aliens were finally at their end point, and some aliens had realised their race wasn't beyond mass violence and they would never change.

So they wanted their whole race to end just to stop the endless cycle of violence, rage and death.

"You want to kill your entire race for what?" I asked.

Aiden stepped in front of me and Jack and two spears pressed hard into him. Not impaling him but it was only a matter of time.

I had to use my superpowers to save us.

"Because our race is cruel and evil and those are two things that have to be erased from the world," the leader said.

I tapped into my influencing superpower and forced all of it into the leader and simply commanded him to let us go.

He laughed. "You think your powers can free you? Your powers have no effect on me. Kill them!"

I leapt backwards.

The aliens charged.

I grabbed Aiden and Jack. I tried to teleport. I couldn't.

Spears flew towards us.

The smell of watermelon, coconut and peaches filled the air.

The furry alien appeared on the ground. He snarled at the wooden aliens.

The air crackled with magical energy. The wooden aliens disappeared.

The leader dived towards us.

His fiery hands reached from the furry alien.

I leapt forward.

Jumping into the air.

Kicking the leader away.

The air crackled with magical energy and the leader disappeared.

Then the little furry alien laughed and smiled at us. "Please forgive the kidnapping Lady Plum,"

A moment later we were all back around the conference table and red leather chairs, the Lord of Tunnels was knocked out cold on the ground and I was stunned as I watched the furry alien transform into a God I knew very, very well.

Paladin, the Goddess of creatures, mammals and birds, appeared in perfectly beautiful human form as she smiled at me and everyone else.

Natalia went over and hugged her like they were best friends and then they started laughing.

"I didn't expect to almost die on the mission," Natalia said.

"Yeah sorry about that Nat, I didn't know how else to convince the old Lord that I was a friend and another alien,"

I waved my hands in the air. "What's going on?"

Natalia laughed hard and I felt the need to grab Jack's and Aiden's wonderfully soft hands.

"Sorry guys," Natalia said, "but every so often the gods like to check up on our experiments and we always hope that they're becoming more peaceful but that doesn't always happen. So when we discovered that the Lord of Tunnels wasn't friendly, we needed a way to give them a final chance,"

"So you get the Lord to kidnap us and see if he wants peace or continues to threaten violence even when his species is about to die," I said.

"Seems a little extreme," Aiden said.

Natalia nodded and bit her lower lip. "I honestly hate this part of the job but it has to be done. These aliens would have attacked us all if they weren't trapped,"

I could sadly understand but it still sucked that an entire species was going to die now because it couldn't resist violence.

"We wanted to bring in you guys because you're so good. If anyone could help save the day and species it would be you three," Paladin said.

I wanted to nod because she was right and we had honestly tried but this species was beyond saving.

Natalia hugged us all. "How about we all get out of this place?"

"Definitely," Paladin, Jack and Aiden said.

"Yeah, but how about we go to the Caribbean and get some nice cocktails in the sun and get some real coconuts and not the odour d'wet alien?"

Everyone laughed and nodded and as we all teleported away, I had to admit that I honestly loved this weird, crazy case because I managed to help out the gods, make a new friend and I was finally going to get to taste real coconuts instead of imagining them because of the smell of a wet alien.

That really was the perfect way to end another crazy, weird day in my wonderful life.

AUTHOR OF AGENTS OF THE EMPEROR SERIES

CONNOR WHITELEY

CREATING ITHANE

A SCIENCE FICTION FAR FUTURE SHORT STORY

CREATING ITHANE

This single event changed the galaxy forever and had the power to doom, save or kill all life.

When people normally say they used to be great, be something or even remotely important, they're lying. They really are. When I was in the Imperial Army fighting on a particularly hard world to pronounce (not that it matters now that it's a lifeless husk), I knew a man that claimed to be a billionaire, the best friend of the glorious Rex and even an inventor.

After spending three years with him in infected mud trenches fighting an enemy he couldn't even understand, I quickly realised that he was a liar, a nobody, a person who was useless and always doomed to die.

You see my name is Ianthe Veilwalker. I don't know why my surname is so weird and futuristic but it works and my parents loved me even as the laser blasts from their Imperial Masters cooked their brains alive. And I did have a good childhood and even when I was serving the Rex in the army I always fought to protect humanity.

That's how I ended up here.

I sat in one of the two corners of my black crystal prison cell that was barely tall enough for me to stand up in. It wasn't wide enough for me to do three steps in any direction and my legs were hardly short.

The entire prison cell was tiny and stunk of blood, corruption and charred flesh so I knew I wasn't the first human to be trapped here.

I had to admit that I really did like the small black crystal dome at the very top of my cell. I didn't doubt for a moment it was what my alien captors were using to watch me. The Dark Keres, the foul humanoid alien race that wanted to resurrect their God of Death, always liked to watch me.

I sort of got the sense that they feared me for some reason and they wanted me dead at all cost, and yet they hadn't tried to kill me just yet. It was weird and strange and I was glad they were next to useless at trying to kill me.

But today felt different.

It wasn't the normal hum, pop and vibration of the air that I now understood to be the life-saving magic that kept the Dark Keres and myself alive. But I felt like someone or something else was watching me and focusing on me like I was about to be picked for something I didn't understand.

Granted I could have just been going mad in this tiny damn prison cell, but that was how the Dark Keres won their psychological wars without even lifting up one of their magical fingers.

You see I had just decided that the Rex was a complete and utter dickhead that only cared about himself and corruption so I went rogue. Me and my squad mates decided to go wrong but the Dark Keres attacked us in our white pod-like shuttle.

We all tried to fight as much as we could but it was useless. The Dark Keres ambushed us and there was nothing we could even remotely do to save ourselves.

I was the only survivor and that was how I ended up in a damn prison cell waiting to die a death that I hoped would come soon. I love humanity, I love life and I want to protect humanity no matter the cost but being in a prison cell just isn't how I want to live.

Someone laughed behind me.

I stood up and noticed how one of the dark crystal walls that trapped me had turned see-through. I stared at the foul, awful Dark Keres with their almost translucent skin, humanoid features and burnt red veins that made him look like a demon.

He smiled at me but I could tell there was no warmth, interest or concern behind those eyes. There was only a lust for murder and pain and my death.

I instantly knew that it was my time to die but knowing the Keres they were certainly not going to make it boring at all.

As the Dark Keres clicked his fingers I felt a fog come over my mind and I collapsed to the ground as my world turned black.

Little did Ianthe know that on the other side of the galaxy a ritual was happening that would change her life and the fate of the galaxy forever.

***

I woke a few moments later and frowned as I found myself in the middle of a massive Colosseum made from the same awful black crystal as my prison cell. It was perfectly smooth, glassy and I just wanted to smash it up, ideally with the skull of a Dark Keres but all I could focus on was the strange ambition of escape.

The Colosseum was immense and I tried to focus on the thousands upon thousands of Dark Keres with their pale skin, awful humanoid features and deranged looks as they focused on me. But I could feel their dark magical energy crackling in the air.

I covered my nose as the air was filled with the horrid aroma of charred flesh, burnt ozone and another more alien smell that I really didn't want to identify.

I had always known that the Dark Keres loved playing games in their Colosseums, and this warband had to be powerful in their hierarchy if they had a Colosseum, but I could feel fear in the air too.

I flat out did not understand how I was now feeling things because this made no sense. I was a normal human woman that wanted to protect, treasure and love life but this ability to actually sense things was just weird.

"See what is about you woman," someone said in a deranged voice.

I shook my head as three human corpses appeared around me

that hadn't been there moments ago. They were all former soldiers like me and they had been completely stripped of armour, weapons and skin as their corpses laid there.

At least I now knew how the Dark Keres dealt with their criminals. They simply killed them in the Colosseums, and the bastards used this for sport and entertainment too. They really were monsters.

"Let us give the Dark Lord Geneitor," someone said, "a game to remember,"

I instantly broke out into a fighting position as I felt the ground vibrate and then a very tall Dark Keres woman appeared. Her white skin glowed dark and magical energy crackled around her.

She had to be a Keres witch corrupted by their God Geneitor to be a mindless instrument of his will.

I so badly wished I had a weapon.

The woman shot out her hands.

Black torrents of fire rushed towards me.

I rolled to one side.

The fire chased me.

The fire turned into dogs.

The dogs chased me.

I ran.

I couldn't allow the fire to touch me.

The witch unleashed more fire.

More dogs formed.

Twenty dogs chased me.

I spun around.

I had to fight death with life.

I charged.

The dogs hesitated.

I didn't.

I leapt into the air.

Kicking a fiery dog in the head.

It died.

Agony shot through my leg.

The dogs charged at me.

I punched them.

Kicked them.

Snapped their bones.

My skin burnt.

My clothes fused to my skin.

The witch made a black fiery sword form in her hand.

She flew at me.

She swung.

Again.

And again.

I ducked.

I rolled.

I fled.

Black magical energy gripped a hold of me.

Throwing me towards her.

I flew towards the witch.

She raised her sword. I grabbed it as I slammed into her.

I thrusted it into her. The witch died.

As soon as the witch's corpse disappeared, the entire damn Colosseum went deadly silent and they all looked to a particular point that I couldn't see. Maybe they wanted to ask their warlord what was going to happen next. Maybe they might give me my freedom.

I seriously doubted it.

"Most impressive human," someone said, "but let us see how you do against the most devout servants of Geneitor,"

I shook my head. "All I want is to live. Protect life. Save people. That is all I want so I don't want to kill you,"

I didn't know why I said that but it just felt right in the moment. But as a massive wolf the size of a shuttle appeared at the other end of the Colosseum I seriously knew that I could never ever reason with the Dark Keres.

The wolf charged.

I went to roll.

I felt a sword at my feet. The same one the witch had used. I grabbed it.

I charged at the wolf.

The wolf charged even faster.

I jumped into the air.

I swung the sword.

The sword shattered as it touched the wolf.

The Dark Keres laughed.

It was deafening.

The wolf chomped down on my leg.

Throwing me about like a rag doll. Breaking my leg. Shattering bone.

The wolf threw me to one side.

I landed with a thud.

I forced myself up. I couldn't use a leg.

The wolf charged.

I tried to run.

I couldn't.

The wolf whacked me to one side.

I smashed into the black crystal.

The wolf roared.

It was playing with me as it slowly came over to me and I realised that I was going to die here. I was going to become just another victim one of the Dark Keres and my soul or whatever it was called would be tortured and devoured by Geneitor, forever.

It was weird because all I wanted to do was protect people, preserve life and make sure that no one ever harmed an innocent person again.

I stared in utter defiance as the wolf came over to me and grinned with an unnaturally human smile as its fangs got closer.

The wolf snapped me in two.

Everyone cheered, laughed and sang happy songs as the life drained from me but I realised that as everything turned white, that I wasn't actually dead yet.

I saw an immense picture of a Keres woman formed but this woman was kind, angelic and I could feel her sheer aura of life, hope and protection. She was inspiring as hell even though I didn't know her and all she made me want to do was get back to my body and defeat the Dark Keres.

"How badly do you want to protect life human?" the woman asked in perfect Imperial tongue.

"With all my being,"

"Will you serve me and become the Daughter of Genetrix?" the woman asked.

I didn't know what she meant but I knew that Genetrix was the Keres Goddess of life, protection and hope. And if Geneitor was real then she had to be real too.

"Definitely," I said with such rage that I hope she knew how angry I was at the Dark Keres for daring to kill me.

"Then return to life Daughter of Genetrix and free me,"

Before I could ask what she meant I felt pure magical energy pour into me and I was flat out amazed at all the Keres knowledge, forbidden texts and divine guidance that was entering my mind. I might not have known everything about the Keres and their gods but that didn't matter for now.

I opened my eyes back in the Colosseum and I shook my head at the Wolf.

Everyone noticed what was happening as they stopped their cheering, singing and laughing. And let me tell you hearing that deafening noise stop was shocking as hell.

I thrusted out my hand and an immense white lightning bolt shot out that killed the wolf so quickly that I had to double-check that it had actually died.

"What is this?" everyone shouted.

I smiled as I felt the love, guidance and protection of Genetrix flow through my veins. "This is the future Dark Keres. Genetrix has touched my soul, given me power and now I will make sure you fail to resurrect Geneitor and wipe out all life in the galaxy,"

"Impossible," someone said. "Geneitor is all-powerful. He has a cult dedicated to him and we will find all the Soulstones needed to bring him down,"

"You might have a head start on us. You might have the resources that we don't. But I am the Daughter and Chosen of Genetrix and I will not allow you to live any longer,"

"Kill her lads,"

I just grinned as the stupid Dark Keres leapt down over the Colosseum's black crystal railings as they charged towards me. I flicked my wrists and two huge white swords formed in my hands. And I was so glad I had specialised in sword combat back in the Imperial Army.

I charged.

I swung.

I sliced.

I diced.

It was a slaughter.

I ripped into the flesh of the enemy.

Throats were slashed.

Chests exploded.

Dark Keres screamed out in agony.

There were too many. Too many Dark Keres for me to kill. They would overwhelm me in short order.

I fell back.

I sensed the Keres were behind me.

I ducked. A sword passed behind me.

I realised I had to keep killing. Keep fighting. Keep living.

I didn't know how I knew. But each death brought me closer to my salvation because Genetrix would help me.

Yet first she needed death to power her creation.

I screamed in rage.

I dived forward.

Swinging my swords.

Slashing throats in bloody arcs.

Ramming my swords into chests.

Unleashing torrents of fire with my mind.

A sword slashed my back.

I froze.

The Dark Keres sliced my arms.

I dropped my swords.

The Keres kicked me to the ground.

They jumped on my head.

I screamed in crippling pain.

I unleashed a fireball.

Killing two Keres.

And that was when it happened.

I felt the veil between this reality and the next become paper thin and then they disappeared.

"Come to me Vita," I said.

An immense deafening roar, scream and shout in a language I didn't know all rolled into one echoed across the planet as a blinding white light appeared above me.

Vita was a demon, a demi-God, a creation by divine power that I could summon and I was more than glad about that.

She was a huge Keres woman with golden magical energy crackling around her.

She screamed out. She launched torrents of white fire. She unleashed all her divine power.

The Dark Keres didn't stand a chance as Vita slaughtered them. The Keres tried to run, tried to flee, tried to scream. It didn't matter as Vita cooked them alive, slaughtered them and scooped up their souls so Genetrix could protect them against the predations of Geneitor.

Within a few moments the slaughter was over and Vita just smiled at me, and I wasn't sure if this was Vita smiling or Genetrix. Maybe she was impressed with what I had done, maybe she was pleased to see her Will made real for a change or maybe she was happy that there was now hope in the galaxy that Geneitor and the Dark Keres might not win after all.

I didn't know what had caused this at all. I didn't know why Genetrix had decided on me as the perfect human or living creature for that now, to become part of her. But I didn't care because for the first time in my life, I actually felt like I had a purpose.

I had always been interested and dedicated to protecting, saving and helping to preserve life and now with Genetrix's power I had the ability to do it. So I bowed to Vita as she disappeared and then it was just me left in the darkness of a former Dark Keres world.

But there was a single rose that grew out of the ground, and that really did make me smile. It showed that even in the most deadly of places, life could and would endure and considering the thousands of Imperial worlds that had been rendered lifeless husks by the Rex's pointless wars, that gave me a hell of a lot of hope for the future.

A future I might not have been certain about, but a future I was really, really excited about because I was Ianthe Veilwalker, human and Daughter of Genetrix.

It was my job to stop the Dark Keres from resurrecting Geneitor no matter the cost.

And that meant the entire galaxy depended on me.

BUM STEALERS

Normally when a former girlfriend calls up and wants to meet with a person they say no, maybe or they say yes so hard that they are basically shouting down the phone at the former girlfriend just so they can prove how much better of a person they are now since their relationship. So when my ex-girlfriend called up apparently needing to talk with me because it was a matter of life or death, well, I couldn't exactly say no but I also couldn't say yes.

Normally I hear about these sorts of difficulties from other people but tonight I was actually sad to experience it for myself. And it just goes to show that sometimes superheroes seriously cannot save everyone.

My name is Matilda Plum, a superhero in the Psychology, Counselling and Therapy part of the world so in normal times I go around helping people, making sure everyone is okay and I help to solve problems. But I never expected to see an ex-girlfriend.

Tonight I was wearing a long sweeping white dress that really helped to show how slim, sexy and fit I was as I sat on a little cold wooden chair in a very posh restaurant in Canterbury, England. There weren't exactly too many posh expensive places in the city because students were hardly that rich, but there were some.

The restaurant was very nice and posh with its massive eating area with brown hardwood floors, massive chandeliers every five metres and crystal cutlery that I was almost scared to touch in case it broke.

The sound of the restaurant was almost deafening with the constant noises of people hitting plates, laughing and shouting at the poor wait staff. It was a nightmare and I was amazed that I had heard of this place through my business contacts. It should have been impossible to conduct business in such a noisy place.

There were plenty of people in here tonight which surprised me, but I was right next to a window giving me a stunning view of Canterbury Cathedral a few tens of metres from me, and there were two other tables within earshot of me. One table was empty but another had a very cute young straight couple. The man was very sexy with his longish blond hair, evil smile and tight blue shirt, and because I could hear them I just knew that the woman was going to get some action tonight.

Sadly I just knew I wasn't.

Especially as when my former girlfriend, Minty Croftford, had phoned me out of breath, clearly distressed and in need of my help, it turned out that I wasn't mature enough to invite her around to my place.

Instead I decided to invite her to the most expensive restaurant in the city, knowing full well she couldn't afford anything on the menu. Maybe that shouted needy, annoying or insecure but I did not care.

"Hi there," Minty said as she pulled herself out a seat without giving me a chance to even offer. Not that I actually wouldn't have offered I wasn't that sort of person.

Minty was still beautiful despite her ageing dramatically since our relationship had ended back in the 90s, and whilst I still looked the same as I did before World War One because superheroes don't age past thirty, her cheeks and body and legs were rounder and thicker, but she still had a beauty to her that I did miss.

Minty had always been a great dresser and she certainly didn't disappoint tonight with her tight-fitting black dress, massive gold earrings and even larger red lips that were very good to kiss back in the day. But there was one thing that was very, very different about her.

Her bum.

Minty had never really had a bum before and there wasn't anything for me to hold when we were together but now, now it might have been big enough to become an independent island.

That was strange.

The entire restaurant smelt heavenly with hints of garlic, tomato and rich Mexican spices that I loved more than anything else in the world but I was here to do a job sadly and not enjoy the food.

"What's wrong?" I asked.

"I think something is trying to steal my ass," Minty said.

With that little comment, I waved over a very cute young male waiter who was wearing a black waiter's uniform that was certainly too small for him but it looked good, and I ordered me and Minty two diet cokes, three pizzas and one order of garlic doughballs to go. Since I knew that my best friends Superheroes Jack and Aiden wouldn't be happy if I had come here without getting them anything.

"Tell me more about this problem," I said very neutrally and channelling my calming and trusting superpowers into Minty. There were times when I loved my superpowers being all the myths and misconceptions about psychologists.

"I can't," she said.

I leant across the table and gently rubbed her hand as a way to tell my superpowers to take it up a notch. I really needed her to trust me if I was ever going to help her.

"At night," Minty said. "three men come into my bedroom and start playing with my ass. They poke it, play with it and kiss it,"

I slowly nodded and decided that she was either lying or she was telling the truth. So I needed to activate another superpower of mine which involved me reading her mind and thankfully because she was talking to me I could access all of her mind.

As I dug into her mind I was amazed that she was actually telling the truth. It was always the same three men every single night and they would always come into her bedroom at three o'clock in the morning, rip off her clothes and bedding and looked at her ass.

Then they would do all the other things I would do it as well.

The thing that seriously confused me though was that these men weren't men in the slightest. They were humanoid for sure but they weren't men or even human and they weren't even aliens.

They were very earthly creatures called the Greys, and before you even start remotely connecting them to the so-called aliens that live in the middle of the Earth. They are not.

The Greys are very nice, kind and friendly people that look like humans, talk like humans and like to build vast underground empires for themselves unlike humans. Yet I couldn't understand why they would want my former girlfriend's ass.

I was going to need some help.

"Jack! Aiden!" I shouted into the air.

Moments later the entire restaurant froze and the sheer silence of the place made me almost jump but it was good seeing Minty frozen mid-sentence and two very cute superheroes pulled over chairs and looked at me.

Both Jack and Aiden were such a cute couple and tonight they were both wearing matching black shiny suits, pink ties and black shoes. They both smelt amazing too with hints of their aftershaves filling the air rather heavily.

"Opera?" I asked.

Jack nodded. "Yeah don't tell me about it,"

Aiden laughed. "You know you love it really. So what you need Matty?"

I just pointed to Minty and told them about the Grey situation and really hoped they knew something I didn't about the Greys.

"Did you know what her butt implants are made from?" Jack asked.

Normal people might have said no but as I was still connected to her mind I double-checked and was surprised to see that Minty (in all her foolishness) had gone to a backstreet surgeon to have the so-called best implants done and I was amazed that she had only had a two-week long infection.

"Backstreet surgeon called *Smiths Butts*," I said.

Jack and Aiden just looked at each other.

"What?" I asked.

Aiden leant across the table like there was actually a chance of us being overheard when they had both frozen us in time.

"Smiths Butts uses very dark procedures and resources to make the implants. And Mr Smith gets the materials for the implants from a Welsh mountain very close to a Grey burial site,"

"Oh," I said.

And that really was all I needed to know, because if the Greys were anything, they seriously liked to honour, create and be extremely respectful to their dead. I once visited them to help improve relations between them, the humans and the Superhero worlds, and I had visited them during their version of the Day of the Dead but for them it's a Year of the Dead.

I don't think I've ever been as drunk as I was then and I only stayed for three hours.

So there was a great chance that Minty's butt implants contained the remains of Greys, since the bodies of Greys dissolved into sand-like particles, and the Greys wanted their dead back.

I just looked at Aiden and Jack because I had no clue how I was going to tell my former girlfriend what I had found out.

"Have fun," the cute boyfriends said before they disappeared and restarted time again. And it was only then that I realised the entire reason for them stopping time was so they wouldn't miss any of their opera show. I almost felt sorry for Jack.

Minty coughed a little and smiled at me. "What do you think? Can you help me?"

I just had to tell her about the Greys, so I did.

Minty laughed so hard that I thought her face was going to crack. "Yeah right. You really are as crazy as I thought back in the 90s,"

I frowned at her. "I'm very serious. If have dead Greys in your butt then they will kill you for it. the Greys honour their dead very seriously,"

"What would they do to me?" Minty asked like this was all still impossible.

"They were rip out your ass," I said. "They will put their slimy hands down your throat, reach down to your bum and pull your implants out. It's the only way they know how to access the human body as they hate cutting things,"

Minty shrugged and stood up. "You always were good at fairy tales,"

"Just have the implants removed. I know many great doctors that would do it without pain, a scar or anything. Please. Just have them removed,"

I really forced my influencing superpowers to open her mind up to the idea.

Minty shot a look at me like I had threatened to kill her. "Fuck off. I am not having my bum removed! If your Greys want my ass they can rip it off me for all I care!"

Minty stormed around and the entire restaurant was staring at me like I was a criminal.

But I wasn't the one that was about to die.

***

I completely respected the right of a person, any person, man or woman, to decide what they did to their own body. I didn't have a problem with that whatsoever but I did have a problem with Minty dying.

Over the next two days, I had called every single superhero I can think of from the Medical Sector, Psychology sector, Boobs, Bums and Cock Sector (and yes that is a real thing) and all I wanted was someone to give me an idea about how I was going to get Minty to change her mind about getting her implants removed.

No luck there.

I had even showed up at her brand-new house on the outskirts of London with its massive bright white walls, perfectly done rose garden and two immense Land Rovers on the driveway. I had knocked on the door and her wife had hugged me and welcomed me inside and then Minty had kicked me straight back out.

Afterwards I decided I had no other option than to get me, Jack and Aiden to constantly phone her home phone and mobile every minute we had in-between helping our clients at my mental health clinic.

That didn't last more than ten minutes because she blocked all our numbers.

I had even decided to go to see the Greys because they loved me for some reason and I had managed to get them to give me two more days to see if I could retrieve their dead relatives without them effectively killing Minty.

The only option I had left was to be unethical and get the implants removed without her consent but I wasn't going to do it, my boss wouldn't allow me to do it and even if I did do it to save her single life, I would never forgive myself.

Because I have been alive since before the first world war and I have seen first-hand the horrific consequences of people not being allowed to decide what they did to their bodies.

So three days later, after trying to see Minty again and getting shot down and causing Minty and her wife to get divorced because the wife believed me, I sat at my large dark brown desk in my therapist room with a wide range of chairs surrounding me and I read the local paper.

Minty had been found dead at the strike of midnight in her house when neighbours had heard her screaming out in agony and they had found her bedsheets wet with blood and her ass was as flat as it was the day she had been born.

As much as I hated what had happened I couldn't really be angry at myself because I had tried everything over the past three to five days (I had been so busy I didn't even know what the day was) but as I still had access to her mind up until she died because I had never shut off the connection, I gave it a final scan.

And I had found something very, very important.

When I have clients with some forms of eating disorders, self-esteem amongst other conditions, I tend to see that they attach a lot of their happiness to a certain part of their body. And it turned out that Minty was obsessed with having a big ass.

She clearly believed that having a big ass would sort out how bad she felt about herself, how she hated her body and how she wanted to feel powerful. But that wasn't how the body, mind or behaviour worked.

I knew for a fact that Minty could have had the world's biggest ass and she never would have been happy and that was sad in a way.

But sometimes as a superhero you really couldn't save everyone, Minty was clearly one of them.

I put the paper in the small black waste bin by my desk and focused on the massive pile of folders on my desk because they were all the clients I was seeing today and these were the people that I could help, save and hopefully they wouldn't end up like Minty.

AUTHOR OF AGENTS OF THE EMPEROR SERIES

CONNOR WHITELEY

RITUAL OF REBIRTH

A SCIENCE FICTION FAR FUTURE SHORT STORY

RITUAL OF REBIRTH

After fighting to protect humanity on hundreds of worlds, after killing more enemies than he cared to remember and after being betrayed by more people than he wanted to think about, Commander Jerico Nelson had never ever expected to be in the employ of the very alien race that he had unfortunately killed out of blind obedience to humanity's monstrous leader known as the Rex.

Jerico wasn't particularly a fan of this strategic position as he stood on the very edge of a massive blood-red crater with gentle slopes. The slopes alone with its near perfectly smooth red rocks made this a bad position to defend. Ideally he would have loved to be in a crater with steep slopes that would slow down the enemies. Yet these awful red slopes wouldn't do anything to make his defence job any easier.

The entire red, sandy, rocky planet wasn't ideal for defence. Jerico wasn't a fan of the massive red mountains in the distance that rose up from the ground like daggers, just waiting to kill him, his men and his alien allies.

He really loved positions that were surrounded by flat ground so he could see his enemies for miles before they actually got within striking distance. But he couldn't help his stomach tighten at the very notion of snipers setting up in the mountains to take him and his men out.

The only major benefit of this crater that was there was a small rocky platform that his alien allies, the Keres, had created for him and his men. At least that way if there was an attack then they could easily hide, jump down and use it as their own snipers' nest.

But Jerico just couldn't help focusing on the stormy sky above them. The blood-red clouds with small amounts of crimson swirled in them really didn't make Jerico feel at ease. The gathering storm looked evil, cold and like it was going to be the death of all of them.

The entire planet smelt of damp sand with the odd hint of gun oil, burnt ozone and charred sage from the ritual that the Keres were hoping to perform in the crater. That made the great taste of roast dinner form on his tongue.

Jerico stepped down onto the rocky platform where the five remaining squad mates of his were all playing cards in their black battle armour. They were smiling, having fun and acting like there wasn't a single danger in the galaxy.

Granted Jerico didn't know if the ritual was going to be attacked. He was simply wanting to be sure because the Keres, or as this cult preferred to be called the Daughter of Genetrix, were paying a lot of Rexes for the job.

He still didn't understand how none of the Keres fractions had any sort of currency and their society was based on need and mutual respect. But these Keres were nice, kind and helpful so Jerico didn't mind not understanding everything about them.

Jerico looked down at the bottom of the crater and just shook his head. The Keres were wearing some kind of strange bright white robe that made them look even more like elves and fairies, because of their pointy features, unnaturally thin humanoid body and their almond-shaped eyes.

They had to be finishing up the preparations because Jerico noticed there were the five red, blue and purple Soul stones that the Keres had been obsessed with for months. Apparently each of the Soul Stones contained a Demi-god belonging to their Goddess of Life Genetrix.

Jerico didn't buy it.

But the Rexes were good and he really wanted to upgrade his

equipment and actually pay his men so he really, really didn't care.

"Commander we are ready," a Keres said in a scarily good impression of Imperial Tongue.

Jerico nodded and he tightened his grip on his machine gun and he gestured that his men should also start to get ready, because if an attack was going to happen then it was going to happen very, very soon.

Jerico watched his men go up to the top of the ridge of the crater and he was about to join them when he caught what was happening with the Keres below.

All of them were holding hands and sitting on the icy cold floor with sharp shards of rock digging into their asses. The five Soul stones were in the middle and they were glowing.

The Keres started singing a beautifully sweet perfect melody that made Jerico want to cry, something he hadn't done in decades and he felt the air crackle, buzz and hum with magical energy around him.

Jerico looked up and frowned as the thunder roared overhead. The violent storm clouds were coming together and Jerico had a very, very bad feeling about this.

It got even worse when an immense spherical warship belonging to the Rex appeared in-between flashes of lightning.

The Imperium was here and they were going to attack.

Jerico went to shout to the Keres but his mouth was frozen and he felt like something was influencing him not to interfere under any circumstances. And for some reason he obeyed.

He rushed up to the top with the rest of his men.

"We have company," Jerico said.

He nodded at Thomas as he checked his pistols and young Allen looked unsure about his third battle but Jerico had faith in all of his men.

A deafening roar screamed overhead as a nuclear bomb was dropped.

Jerico wanted to scream like the rest of his men but he knew they would be okay for now. The Goddess Genetrix would protect them and as soon as the nuclear bomb touched the top of an invisible dome the sheer extreme impact was reflected.

Jerico's mouth dropped as he saw the sheer destructive power of the bomb rip the Imperial vessel limb from limb.

A Keres screamed in agony.

The storm clouds smashed into each other.

The thunder roared.

It screamed.

It screamed bloody murder.

Jerico's ears started to bleed.

Black lightning shot down around them.

Jerico jumped to one side.

The ritual was starting now and Jerico knew that it flat out couldn't be undone. Something was happening not in this reality but Jerico understood in a way he didn't understand that his life was about to change forever.

A furious roar echoed around the planet as Jerico saw two white pod-like shuttles were flying towards them. Some damn humans from the Imperial ship had survived.

Jerico clocked that the two shuttles were splitting up.

Jerico grabbed Thomas and Allen and he took them to the other side of the crater.

The shuttle landed with a crash and Jerico aimed his gun at the door of the pod-like shuttle. He wanted, needed to kill these humans to protect whatever was going on.

The shuttle doors exploded open.

The Imperial army soldiers exploded out.

Firing as they went.

Jerico fired back.

Bullets slammed into Jerico's armour.

He stood firm. He couldn't be defeated.

He fired controlled shots.

Bullets screamed through the air.

Smashing into the enemy's faces.

Heads exploded.

Skulls shattered.

Thomas's head imploded.

Jerico ran backwards.

More high-velocity shots screamed at him.

Jerico spun around.

There were snipers in the mountains.

Jerico ran over the ridge of the crater with Allen.

They charged at the soldiers.

Cutting them down.

Jerico unleashed the full power of his gun.

He slaughtered the enemy.

The shuttle exploded.

Throwing them forward.

Jerico slowly forced himself up and he was so glad that he was okay. All the enemies in the shuttle were dead and that him and Allen could now go and reinforce the other position but the storm screamed in terror overhead.

Jerico looked over to Allen's unmoving body and he went over to it. Allen's eyes were glassy and cold and lifeless as Jerico noticed all the metal shards from the shuttle covered his body.

The storm roared overhead.

The wind was howling all around him creating immense sandstorms.

Jerico could barely see where he was going so he allowed his instincts to guide him.

He made his way round the crater but he was annoyed as hell he could no longer hear the gunshots and screaming of the Imperial soldiers. He really hoped that his men were okay.

He couldn't lose them. They had to live. Just had to.

Jerico found his way to the other side and he frowned at the three remaining dead bodies of his men. The other Imperial shuttle had exploded and the mountain in the distance shattered as a lightning bolt from the storm smashed into it.

"Help Genetrix!" a Keres shouted at the top of her lungs.

The storm grew even more intense.

Jerico ran up the crater.

Lightning bolts hammered the ground.

Jerico leapt to one side.

Then another.

Then another.

Lightning bolts were everywhere.

Immense chunks of mountain rock fell down around him.

Jerico ran away from the crater.

The chunks of rock hammered the ground.

And then Jerico went down the crater as fast as he could but he already knew it was way, way too late to save anyone.

As the storm screamed a final time and unleashed vast amounts of magical energy into the atmosphere that scorched Jerico's lungs and made him scream out in agony, Jerico collapsed to his knees as he saw what the hell had happened.

All the Soul Stones were gone now and where they had once been was littered with the corpses of humans and Keres alike. A lot of the rock inside the crater was charred and smouldering so Jerico had no idea what had caused that.

But he had failed.

It was Jerico's job to protect his men, protect the Keres and make sure that whatever had happened today was going to happen without a single problem. He was nothing but a failure.

Jerico had no idea how he was going to contact the families, friends and loved ones of his proud wonderful men that had died under his command. He couldn't tell the families any of the details because it was illegal for humans to work with the Keres but he wanted to help the victims of this attack somehow.

Jerico saw something move below him.

Jerico slowly went down into the crater with his machine gun ready to fire if needed. The entire crater smelt awful of charred flesh, burnt ozone and another strange burnt smell that was probably to do with the sheer amount of magic in the air.

"You live," a female Keres said in her blood soaked and blackened robes.

Jerico rushed over to her and held her in his arms. He applied pressure to the wound but it was still flowing too quickly. She was going to die and it would be all his fault.

"I'm sorry I failed," Jerico said.

The woman laughed. "You did not fail Son of Genetrix. This outcome was already predetermined by the Goddess and this has the potential to save or doom all life in the galaxy,"

"I don't understand,"

"Humans never do," the woman said. "The Goddess works in magical ways. She came to me with the last of her power a century ago so I could find the Soulstones and Rebirth her so she may walk amongst the stars like she did millions of years ago,"

"But I failed you," Jerico said.

"This is not the right time for Genetrix to return," the woman said. "And now know that I was not the one to Rebirth her. There is a human woman called Ithane Veilwalker, she is the true Daughter of Genetrix,"

Jerico wasn't sure. Why the hell would a Keres Goddess want to have a mere human as her chosen.

"You must find her, protect her and keep her safe. She has just been reborn herself and you must find her. It is only through her that Geneitor is defeated and life in the galaxy will continue. Will you do that for me?"

Jerico nodded because he flat out hated the feeling of her warm blood oozing all over his hands as he failed yet again to save her life.

"Good," the woman said grinning. "Then take my necklace too. The Goddess was clever and she showed me the way. Take the necklace and may the Soulstone of Spero, Goddess of Hope, guide you like it has me,"

Jerico was about to question it. He couldn't be entrusted with such an important task, he was a failure, he was nothing, he was a mere human. But the female Keres died in his arms and he simply took off the golden necklace with the weird blue crystal at the end of it, and smiled.

He had no idea what the future was going to offer. The future could have been dark horrid and filled with suffering for all he knew but he had his mission and he had his destiny already laid out for him.

He wasn't sure that any human truly understood what intergalactic and maybe even interdimensional game of God and Goddess they were all blindly entering into, but that didn't matter. Because he was going to find this Ithane woman, he was going to find the Soulstones once more and he was going to succeed this time.

And bring down Geneitor once and for all.

All because he had hope for a better future, a better life and hopefully redemption for allowing all the amazing people around him to die, when they really didn't need to.

AUTHOR OF AGENTS OF THE EMPEROR SERIES

CONNOR WHITELEY

BATTLE DOCTRINES

A SCIENCE FICTION SPACE OPERA SHORT STORY

BATTLE DOCTRINES

Ship Mistress Olivia Flapper stood on her raised metal platform in the middle of her white spherical bridge on her great warship *Rex's Hammer*. She had always wanted to be a Ship Mistress, a great leader of the Imperium's war efforts and now after so many years of service, fighting and political workings she was finally one of them.

The bridge was still brand-new to Olivia but it was as wonderful as she ever could have imagined. She really liked the spherical shape of the walls, its smooth white metal was a little too shiny in places but she would sort it all out in time.

Her small raised platform was only big enough for her to stand on which was absolutely perfect, especially as Olivia wasn't a fan of the constant smells of body odour, sweat and blood that seemed to pour off her command crew like rain from a duck. It wasn't exactly pleasant.

At least the small bright golden orbs of light bounced around the bridge, bouncing from one wall to another and back again.

Sometimes when Olivia was alone (which wasn't as often as she would have liked) she just stared at the little orbs. Sometimes they were happier, freer and more content with life than she was.

As much as Olivia loved her new position, her service to the Rex and her life, she just felt like there was more to life than always searching for the next promotion and intensely studying the next battle doctrine that old men with no military experience had created.

The circular warship hummed loudly and Olivia looked down at her command crew, all twenty of them, as they were hunched over their large bulky metal computer screens having to have computations by hand, having to calculate their trajectory by hand and having to inform different departments of the warship by hand.

This certainly wasn't the most modern ship she had ever been on but it was customary for all brand-new Ship Masters and Mistresses to get put on the lowest ships first of all. Apparently it was so they could develop their skills, but Olivia knew it was because the new ones were the most likely to die so it was cheaper to put them on poorer ships before "gifting" them the more expensive warships.

She wasn't really a fan of that rule.

Olivia waved at her command crew as they walked about or did their work wearing their long white robes denoting their position and their newness to the role. It was a shame that Olivia was surrounded by newbies judging by their bright white robes without a single speck of dirt on them.

Either they were so new that they had only graduated from the academy in the past two days or the environmental systems were *so* good that they seriously purified the air.

Judging by the rest of the ship, Olivia fully believed it was the former.

"Ship Mistress, we're detecting three enemy ships incoming. Within firing distance in five minutes," a very short man said with a balding head.

Olivia nodded slowly and her hands tightened around the cold metal railings of her raised platform. She had been sent here on this mission to deliver bombs to a faraway planet to help Imperial forces annihilate a rogue cult of Dark Keres, but clearly the enemy didn't want these bombs delivered.

She had no idea what separated the Dark Keres to the rest of their foul, magic freaks of their Keres species. The Treaty of Defeat was such a weak little treaty that might have meant the awful Keres species was starving itself to death but the Dark Keres were awful.

Unlike the normal Keres, these so-called Dark Keres actually had a spine and they were fighting back against the righteousness of humanity. It was humanity's Rex-given right to rule the stars, purge entire species and claim all the planets they wanted.

And it was the Keres's duty to die or at least join humanity as slaves as so many of their foul kind had.

Olivia focused on the icy coldness of space dead away from them as two large holographic screens appeared showing Olivia the endless blackness of space with no nearby planets, imperial forces or stars close by.

They were alone.

Olivia really didn't want to fight these Dark Keres because they might have been breaking the law time after time but they were just trying to do what they could to survive.

Humanity was constantly doing questionable things to make sure it survived, so maybe the Keres' weren't so different from them after all.

"Battle Doctrine Mistress," a very tall woman said.

Olivia bit her lip as she couldn't even see the foul enemy ships yet, she didn't know what Dark Keres ships looked like but she was going to have to proceed as her training suggested she should.

"Advancement Battle Doctrine," Olivia said.

As the bridge became a hive of activity with her command crew running round like headless chickens, she had to admit it wasn't her favourite Doctrine.

The Advancement Doctrine was sadly all about travelling quickly through space to make sure the enemy couldn't catch up with them. It meant deactivating the weapon systems to give the engines more power but hopefully it would still work.

Olivia really wanted to see the enemy but she just couldn't.

The Keres were masters of their magic and it was so damn annoying that they were probably using it to cloak their ships. For all Olivia knew they could be right next to them.

"How did you know the Keres were here in the first place?" Olivia asked.

None of the command crew were paying attention to her as the warship hummed, banged and vibrated as the engines were given more power. She hated this.

Olivia had fought the Keres plenty of times and whilst the Dark Keres might be different to the rest of their race, she was still willing to bet that they used the same or similar tactics.

The Keres were waiting to ambush them and she feared that the Advancement Doctrine was exactly what they wanted.

"We found them on the edge of the system for a brief second before they cloaked themselves," a woman said as she rushed past.

Olivia nodded but it made no sense. The Keres knew that they couldn't outgun, beat or destroy an Imperial warship because they were so weak, so why in the Rex's fine name did they reveal themselves?

Unless it was all part of a plan.

It was moments like this that just made Olivia want to jump into Ultraspace and zoom through the galaxy at light speed regardless of how apparently dangerous that was with the bombs.

She just wanted to keep her crew alive, and herself of course.

"Scan the surrounding area," Olivia said.

Only one man looked up at her but he shrugged as he ran the scan and then shook his head at her.

Olivia's heart pounded in her chest. She was used to dealing with impossible humans, impossible tasks and impossible crew members. She wasn't used to dealing with impossible aliens.

She didn't want her crew to die. She didn't want to fail. She had to deliver the bombs to the planet over ten hours away.

Then Olivia realised that sometimes the Keres did a little trick where they magically project their ships into space to make the Imperium believe they were in one location when they were actually in another.

The enemy was a lot closer than Olivia ever wanted to admit.

Then Olivia felt her skin turn icy cold and she had only ever had that reaction once. Seconds before the Keres attacked her in the most violent way possible.

"Invasion Doctrine!" Olivia shouted.

But it was too late.

The ship jerked.

Throwing Olivia across the bridge.

Other crew members smashed around her.

Bodies shattering.

Streaks of blood painting the walls.

Alarms screamed overhead.

Flashing lights exploded on.

Olivia forced herself up. She forced herself towards her raised platform.

Her body screamed in protest but she accessed her private hologram.

She saw thousands of victims all over the ship from the impact. A bomb had hit their starboard side but their shields were intact and their anti-magic systems were okay.

At least the Keres couldn't teleport or board them for now.

The two massive holograms that showed her the darkness of space earlier now showed three immense dagger-like warships with blood red crystal hulls appear next to her.

Olivia couldn't believe that the damn Dark Keres were right next to them. That was the last thing she wanted.

She had to somehow figure out a way to keep herself and her crew alive and how to get the bombs to the battlefleet.

For the briefest of moments Olivia supposed she could activate the bombs right now and just kill them all and the Keres warships next to her. But she didn't want to use the No Hope Doctrine just yet.

She wouldn't dare give the alien abominations some reward for their attack. Olivia was going to win no matter what it took.

"Mistress," a voice said but Olivia didn't bother to see who it was. "The Keres want to contact us. They're requesting we surrender to them,"

Olivia shook her head. These damn aliens were never going to get her to surrender.

Olivia forced herself upright and she gripped the metal railings of her raised platform and frowned at the two holographic screens showing the enemy warships.

"We need to activate the weapon systems immediately," Olivia said.

"It will do us no good. The enemy are on the starboard side and our weapons on that side are destroyed," a man said.

Olivia couldn't believe how damn infuriating these aliens were. And the man was right sadly.

A loud humming of pure magical energy crackled around her and Olivia rolled her eyes as the damn anti-magic systems were failing. It wouldn't be too long now until the Keres invaded and slaughtered them all like the beasts they were.

Olivia opened a ship-wide communication channel. "All forces this is the Ship Mistress enact the Containment Doctrine immediately. Do not allow a witch to live,"

Olivia just shook her head even more as her command crew all bit their lower lip. They all knew this was bad because if the anti-magic generators collapsed then the Keres would easily rip into reality and stalk the holy halls of their warship.

And they would kill human after human until they all died.

The Containment Doctrine was simple but useless. A simple hell mary to throw into the air to buy Olivia some more time.

"What about the engines?" Olivia asked.

A young woman from the crew stepped forward. "Contained by Keres. They're using our magic to immobilise them. I could undo the magic but it would take time,"

"How much?"

"Ten minutes," she said.

The air crackled and murderous screams echoed around the ship.

"Do it," Olivia said to the woman before turning to her crew. "Connect me to Keres ships. I'll buy us some time. Weapons won't free us here. Words might,"

Olivia could literally feel the tension in the bridge now and she wanted to slice it with a sword but she had to focus and remain strong. Some Keres creatures only needed eye contact to use their magic.

Olivia had to focus and not allow the abominations to use their magic on her.

Moments later a very tall, thin elf-like woman appeared in blue holographic form with very long golden black hair that flowed around her like angelic wings.

"You must hand over your weapons please my friend," the woman said. "My forces want to unleash their Death Magic on you but I am buying you time,"

Olivia grinned. The woman's voice was very elegant, lyrical and perfect but she was just stupid. Olivia was a Ship Mistress of the Imperium, she did not listen to the lies and deceits and corruption that aliens spread.

And she wasn't going to give them anything.

As soon as the engines were free once more she was going to escape and jump into Ultraspace and to hell with the consequences.

"I will not give you a damn thing alien. These bombs will reach the planet and they will be dropped on your kind and then humanity will rule the stars," Olivia said.

She wasn't exactly sure if she believed it and she didn't know if the Keres on the planet deserved to die but she wanted to act tough at least.

Olivia noticed the female Keres was looking at someone else probably behind the hologram then the female Keres nodded.

"Then you leave me no choice and I know your workers are trying to free the engines," she said.

The entire command crew went still but Olivia waved them to continue.

"Let me show you just a touch of our Death Magic," the woman said before uttering strange twisted words in a tongue Olivia didn't understand or care to listen to.

Olivia cut the transmission but when she looked back at her command crew they were all wide-eyed with terror as they stared back at their computer screens.

Olivia climbed down and looked at the silent ghostly pictures of their friends, fellow crew members and even loved ones turn to black crystal before shattering into dust.

"Two percent of the crew is dead," someone said but Olivia didn't care who.

"Are the engines free?" Olivia asked.

"Almost," a woman said.

Olivia climbed back up to her raised platform and contacted the Keres warships again.

"Did you like my gift? I know the Goddess of Souls was particularly happy," the female Keres said.

Olivia's hands formed fists. She seriously didn't care for the strange alien mythology of the Keres.

The air charged with magic energy and Olivia felt the icy coldness of the Keres's foul touch around her. They were within striking distance.

She just had to buy her crew a little more time.

"Does your Goddess love Keres souls?" Olivia asked.

The female Keres laughed. "Souls are souls my dear. I'll let you meet her now. Because now you die!"

An alien claw formed in the air.

Slashing at Olivia.

She stumbled back.

The claw chased her.

Olivia leapt off her platform.

She smashed onto the floor.

The claw lashed at her.

Olivia rolled forward.

Another claw appeared in front of her.

Olivia jumped to one side.

She hit a table.

The two claws flew at her.

The ship jerked.

The engines were free.

"Into Ultraspace!" Olivia shouted.

The entire ship screamed in protest.

The Keres were trying to anchor them into reality.

Olivia whipped out her pistol.

She shot the two claws.

They disappeared.

The warship zoomed off into Ultraspace and all Olivia could think about was how badly she didn't want the bombs to explode.

***

Olivia absolutely had to admit that the next hour was the longest one of her entire life, each second she was half-expecting one of her crew to shout that the bombs were overheating or somehow having a reaction to Ultraspace travel.

Thankfully they weren't.

Olivia just smiled as she leant against the warm metal railings of her raised platform and watched as the streaks of purple light from the Ultraspace network tunnel (she really didn't know how it worked) zoomed past her.

Then with a quiet thud the tunnel disappeared and Olivia was so damn happy that she was alive and that her crew were okay. Then the entire ship hummed a little as an Imperial network connected to her ship and took control of the bombs.

For a small moment Olivia thought that the Dark Keres had followed her but everyone knew that the Keres were too dumb to use Ultraspace and they stuck with their clearly inferior Nexus System of their own magical creation.

Olivia didn't know how it worked and she didn't want to know. The Keres were dumb, end of story.

And as she watched on the two massive holograms the Imperial fleet zooming around an orange green planet with Keres ships trying to flee, she grinned as the bombs rushed towards the planet ready to be used exactly where they were needed most.

Olivia still wasn't sure if this was just, needed or even right but she hadn't examined the facts of the battle and in all fairness it hadn't mattered.

As much as she didn't like to admit it, the military wasn't designed to produce thinkers, it was designed to produce soldiers that could pick up a gun and march to the beat of the Rex's eternal war machine so humanity could be kept safe, secured and all the enemies could be killed.

The laughter, cheering and even some happy dances filled the bridge as the command crew and everyone else on the ship was so happy to be alive and Olivia was definitely going to join them later on.

She might have doomed a lot of aliens to death but she had helped to protect humanity, her crew and the future of the Imperium. That was certainly a job very well.

And with thousands of other battlefields spread out across the galaxy, Olivia was really excited about flying away from here and seeing what other great adventures, herself, her crew and her great lower warship could travel to.

Then maybe, just maybe Olivia could finally get a promotion and get a real warship because as she had survived this adventure Olivia was fairly sure she could survive anything.

And that was a great realisation to have and that was all thanks to her battle doctrines.

DYING RIGHT

When the strangest request of my professional life happened I was actually at a university fundraiser, it was a wonderful night and I love occasions like this. Partly because they always happen in posh university halls with stunning white walls with little raised decorative moulding to give the walls some texture. The food is always brilliant and the company is nearly always sexy.

I have to admit this was one of those occasions where the company was not up to the normal level of sexiness.

I was standing with my two best friends in the entire world Jack and Aiden, who looked amazing in their matching three-piece suit of black trousers and waistcoats, white shirt and a very cute pink tie. They looked way better than me with my metallic blue blouse and trousers.

If it sounds like I looked awful it's because I was. It was a new fashion look I was trying out and it was so badly failing.

Anyway, the university fundraiser was done rather well in their large white hall, there were tons of people in their best flowery, pink and dark blue dresses with their finest jewellery, walking about. Their husbands and boyfriends were all wearing suits.

There was one particular elderly woman who had to be a billionaire judging by her pearl earrings, necklace and she had a face like a slapped ass. She looked moody so I was avoiding her.

At least me, Jack and Aiden were only here because as superhero psychologists we were consulting with Kent University on their clinical psychology module so they wanted to know what we would have liked to learn about mental health as students.

The problem was of course we never went to university. We got all our psychology knowledge from being a superhero and our boss Natalia, so the consulting gig was interesting to say the least. Thankfully we managed to tell the head of the School of Psychology exactly what he wanted to hear so we got invited to a fancy party.

All the other guests were talking, laughing and commenting on the *amazing* work each of them did to champion their almighty cause.

I'm sorry but half of these people, no in fact all of these people wouldn't know what real work looked like even if it came up and chomped on their assess.

"Why are we here exactly?" Jack asked as he passed me another glass of champagne.

I knew he didn't like parties very much and to be honest neither did I. Or I at least didn't like these posh, snobby parties too much because being a superhero in the psychology, counselling and therapy sector of the world did mean I had to go to them from time to time.

To keep up appearances at the very least.

Danger.

I jumped as the word slammed into my mind and I immediately looked at Jack and Aiden who looked concerned about me. They hadn't heard it but they knew I was reacting to something.

"Someone or something just shouted *danger* into my mind," I said.

"Matilda Plum," a voice said from behind me.

I turned around and found someone hugging me tight before I even managed to see who it was. When the man stepped around he was grinning at me like I was his best friend in the entire world.

Serious Danger.

I tensed as soon as the words entered my mind and I tapped into my superpowers. Thankfully all my powers came from the myths and misconceptions surrounding psychologists so I could easily read this man's mind.

I was shocked when I saw that the man thought he was going to die in the next three hours and he wanted my help making sure he died right and justly. As if I knew what that meant.

I took a large swig from my champagne flute and really focused on the man. He seemed normal, he didn't look not-unattractive in a suit but I wouldn't sleep with him. I doubted Jack and Aiden even would.

"Why do you think you'll die in the next three hours?" I asked.

Jack and Aiden took a few steps closer after taking three small strawberry tarts from a cute waitress.

The man frowned at me. "I just know in three hours the aliens will come for me and kill me. I want your help in preparing my wife for the death,"

I searched his mind again and he honestly believed in this strange story. He believed this story with every single fibre of his being.

This wasn't a joke to him.

"I know you and your friends have *special* skills in this area and you can influence people. Don't worry your boss told me," the man said.

I turned from the man briefly and looked at Jack and Aiden. They hardly seemed convinced but I believed him a little bit. I believed he thought he was going to die, and after all of my alien adventures in the past few months I doubted he was lying about that too.

But why did he want me to help him tell his wife?

"I also know you can teleport us to my wife now," the man said.

I searched for the man's name and he was called John Smith, a normal name if there ever was one.

"What do you think?" I asked my best friends.

Jack looked at his boyfriend and frowned. I loved it how these two put each other on the spot at times. They were brilliant like that.

"Fine. Let's hear him out," Aiden said.

I looked back at the grinning man and I teleported us all out of the party. Just grateful that my superpowers would make everyone think we simply walked out the front door.

I just hoped this wasn't going to be a deadly case. But only one single phase repeated in my mind as we teleported off.

Death Comes.

***

A few moments later we all reappeared inside a very nice living room with a beautiful collection of landscape paintings on the cream walls. They had to be worth about a million pounds each, the cream carpet was soft and spongy so it had to be brand-new and there was a woman sitting there stunned.

The woman was probably middle-aged, stunning and I loved her deep dark sapphire eyes.

She was reading a magazine on fishing (and I forced myself not to judge her too harshly) and I smiled at her. That only made her frown.

The living room smelt of chicken curry and the cars driving up and down the road outside was almost deafening. It was like living right next to a motorway. This must have been awful.

As much as I wanted to talk to the woman she didn't seem friendly, she only seemed annoyed, irritated and like we were invaders or just another part of her husband's crazy plans.

"Not more of your superhero gang," the woman said.

Now she had spoken to me, Jack and Aiden searched her mind and we were surprised that our boss Natalia had had dinner with them three times over the years after they helped her save people. The woman, Naomi, was a firefighter and John was a doctor on weekdays and a surfer at weekends.

They loved each other but I don't know why they weren't too happy with each other right now.

"You aren't going to die John," Naomi said.

"I am," John said.

Jack waved his arms in the air. "Why do you think you're going to die in the next three hours?"

"The old slime ball cheating on me. Fucking a nurse, aren't you? How many little nurses are you pounding away you old dog?" Naomi asked.

I smiled. I didn't want to be involved in a domestic but I could tell this was going to be way too entertaining to miss.

"I am not pounding a nurse," John said.

"No you always were too crap in bed for pounding. You were all like gentle strokes and tickles instead of all flash and bang," Naomi said.

Wow. That was brutal.

I stepped forward and clapped my hands together. "Let's say for a moment you aren't cheating on your wife and want to escape her. Why do you think death is around the corner?"

John shook his head and sat down on the sofa. "Because I just know. For the past two years I have been having the exact same dream that tonight aliens will come for me. My human life will be over and they will take me into the stars,"

So he wasn't exactly going to die but I didn't want to point that out.

"Then," John said, "when I was helping out your boss save the lives of a suicidal man she confirmed the dream was a vision and that it would happen. It's part of the Cyder Pact,"

I gasped.

I wasn't the history buff of our team, that was normally Jack and Aiden, but every superhero knew about the Cyder Pact.

Two thousand years ago a spider-like race of aliens came to the solar system and threatened to invade it totally unless the Gods and Goddesses allowed the Cyder to take a single human every year like clockwork.

There could be no interference in who was chosen or a war would develop and the Gods knew the war couldn't be won at all.

The war would annihilate humanity, or at least kill all the superheroes and Gods just to save what was left of humanity. It would be worse than the End Times.

"I understand," I said to Jack and Aiden.

I understood why the voice was contacting me, it was a Cyber, telling me to not be in the same room as John when he was taken because all witnesses to the taking were also taken. It was a warning to save me.

And now I had to tell Naomi that what her husband was saying was true and that she wouldn't have a body to bury. He would die with no way for her to remember him.

It almost seemed cruel that I had to let John be taken and Naomi would have to suffer like he had actually died. But she would know that he wasn't dead he just could never ever come home to her again.

That got me thinking.

I looked at Jack and Aiden. "What if we convince her and implant the suggestion that John is actually dead?"

Jack and Aiden shook their heads.

Naomi stood up. "What are you saying? My husband is not dying tonight. You cannot convince me otherwise,"

I took Naomi by the hand and we both sat down on the sofa and I didn't dare look at her. This was one of the hardest conversations I've ever had to do.

"Naomi, your husband is going to die tonight in a way. He's going to be taken by aliens to save humanity as part of a peace deal made thousands of years ago,"

Naomi laughed and shook her hands free. "You're all crazy. My husband isn't dying. I am staying with him no matter what,"

"No!" John said in fear.

He knelt down on the floor begging with his wife through tears not to be in the same room as him.

I searched his mind and I realised he had seen this version of the night play out. She would be in the same room as him and she would also be taken.

They had three great children together, all studying at university to become a lawyer, doctor and a psychologist (a very good choice), and they loved their parents more than anything in the world.

John knew, truly knew if both of them were gone then their kids would be orphaned, there would be no family left and the kids would struggle to finish university. John had written up a great will for them so they were more than taken care of but it wasn't the point to him.

Their adult children still needed a parent.

Each adult child had a boyfriend or girlfriend and John's biggest concern was who would walk the two girls down the aisle and who would help their son prepare for the wedding.

I completely agreed.

I shared all of this through a mental link with Jack and Aiden and they still shook their heads.

"It's our job to save people not convince them their husband's died," Jack said.

"But we need to protect her mental health," Aiden said sort of on the fence about my plan.

"Exactly. What's worse for her? Convincing yourself your husband might return from space. Or knowing your husband is dead and having a chance of moving on,"

I hated the words as they came out of my mouth but they were true. So damn true that I hated this.

"Fine," Jack said smiling. He knew this was the only course of crazy action.

We all interlocked our fingers and stared at Naomi so there was no chance our influencing superpower would fail.

We coursed through her mind and implanted the suggestion and series of memories to support it that John had died from a heart attack that night in the kitchen, the paramedics had raced here but he was already dead.

We then expanded our influencing superpower so everyone on the street remembered seeing an ambulance appear and then later on a black one to take the body away. I personally added the suggestion for everyone to pop in and check on Naomi over the next week to support her.

It felt so damn wrong doing this and I knew our boss was watching us so she would contact the Gods of the medical world to fake the post-mortem results and create a fake body for the family to bury.

Then Naomi went to the sofa, sat down and stared into space as the suggestions continued to take effect.

"Thank you so much. I love my family and wife so damn much," John said crying as he left the living room.

I knew we were approaching the three-hour mark. We had to act.

John was in the bathroom so I simply closed my eyes as did Jack and Aiden and I heard the tapping of creatures moving about in the bathroom I forced myself not to run in there and save him.

It was him or damn the entire human race.

I hated that choice but I would hate humanity being wiped out even more.

***

Two weeks later, I wore a long black sweeping dress to the funeral and Jack and Aiden both hugged each other tight as we watched the funeral from afar. It was a packed funeral, easily two hundred men and women in their black hats, suits and dresses.

I had a feeling that John would have liked this, it was a touching service and it really did focus on how amazing his life was.

Everyone was walking past the rows upon rows of headstones with a dark little church in the background, all three kids were devastated but I had sent little suggestions into their minds to help give them strength, courage and to make sure they knew how much their father loved them.

They seemed a little better when they left but they were grieving a lot. Naomi was stronger than I had thought and she seemed to take comfort in how she had gotten a chance to bury her husband.

I had briefly scanned her mind during the service and she didn't know me, Jack or Aiden but she didn't question us. She avoided us more than anything else and she seemed at peace.

As Naomi's black SUV drove off, I hugged my best friends in the entire world because we had done a lot over the past two weeks. We had all allowed humanity to survive, a husband to be taken without being burdened about their family and we had helped a family a little.

They would be grieving for ages at the death of their dad but at least they now had a chance to recover, move on and find happiness again without wondering if and when their father would ever return from space.

And if that wasn't dying and doing right then I didn't want to know what more a great father could do for the family he loved.

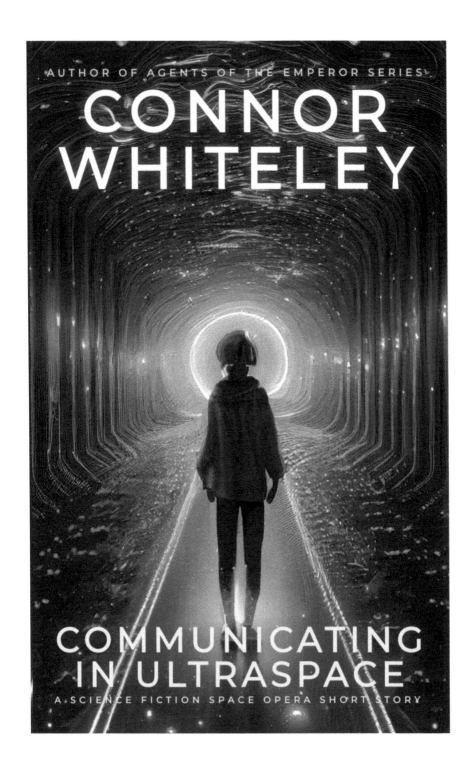

AUTHOR OF AGENTS OF THE EMPEROR SERIES

CONNOR WHITELEY

COMMUNICATING IN ULTRASPACE

A SCIENCE FICTION SPACE OPERA SHORT STORY

COMMUNICATING IN ULTRASPACE

This was the day he died.

Chief Communication Officer Grayson Jones sat on a large grey metal table that was surprisingly smooth, shiny and very relaxing oddly enough. It was almost strange for a table in his little metal boxroom of a break room to be so relaxing and well-maintained. Normally when he worked on ships the breakrooms were so dilapidated that they were just flat out disgusting.

Thankfully everything about the brand-new black circular ship imaginatively called the *Communication* was up to date, clean and perfectly maintained. Grayson had already been on the ship for two weeks and he had yet to find a single problem with the ship.

The only problem with the ship was that it was the smooth walls of the break room were just so plain and dull. Grayson wanted to splash some colour on the walls and maybe hang a few pictures. A nice red, blue or orange might have looked nice and it would be a nice reminder of his homeworld.

Grayson really liked that idea as he wrapped his rough hand around his coffee mug, the sharp bitter taste of it was one of the highlights of living on the ships. And it helped to provide a brief distraction against the overwhelming aromas of roasted peaches, sweat and salted peanuts that clung to everything in the corridor amongst the ship.

He didn't know why the environmental systems were so obsessed with the smell, they could have been faulty, but it was rather nice at first before getting old real quick.

At least the job was simple enough, he was just in charge of making sure all the equipment ran smoothly so all the nearby Imperial forces could route their communications through his station, before the ship blasted the messages off through Ultraspace towards their destination.

Ultraspace was amazing and Grayson really loved learning about it at university. It was just stunning how humanity had managed to create or tap into an intergalactic network of tunnels that allowed for faster-than-light travel.

It was simply brilliant.

And the only thing Grayson needed to do was keep it all working otherwise he absolutely hated to imagine what would happen if he failed. Battle orders might not be read or sent, distress calls might not be heard and vital intelligence might not be known about aliens and terrorists.

If Grayson failed then he sadly knew a lot of good people could die and there was no way he was ever allowing himself to have that on his conscious. He didn't volunteer for five years in the Peace Corps to allow innocent people to die.

"We have a problem," a woman said as a large circular door opened with an annoying screaming sound that almost made Grayson jump.

He looked at the Chief of Engineering, a beautiful woman called Mary wearing a very attractive pink blouse, trousers and white trainers.

But if she was coming to him then it had to be bad.

"What happened this time?" Grayson asked grinning.

"The Ultraspace generator died," Mary said plainly.

Grayson just shook his head. Of all the damn things that could possibly go wrong, he seriously didn't want this to be the problem.

Without their Ultraspace generator then the ship couldn't run away or travel through the network basically increasing their travel time by a factor of 100 and that meant the Ultraspace Communicator would fail sooner or later too.

Grayson had sadly worked too many jobs where the failing of the Ultraspace generator wasn't seen as the first sign of an Ultraspace shutdown on the ship so when the damn aliens attacked. There was no way of escape or call for help.

Those people always died.

"And there's ten Keres ships two systems over. The great benefits of invading their territory," Mary said.

Grayson seriously didn't want to attract the attention of the foul alien beasts with their awful magic. He wanted to escape in short order and he hardly agreed with Mary about space being the Keres' domain. The stars belonged to humanity and only humanity.

"I presume you've tried turning it on and off?" Grayson asked.

Mary playfully hit him over the head. "I didn't come to you to get mocked. This is a communicator error, the Ultraspace Communicator is *telling* the Generator to shut down,"

Grayson leant forward. He had heard a hell of a lot of things in his decades of service as a soldier fighting the Keres and then even more as a communication specialist. He had never heard of pieces of the ship *telling* each other what to do.

He wasn't even sure if the Keres's magic could do such things to Imperial ships.

"Take me there immediately please," Grayson said.

He was surprised at how hesitant Mary was to let him go but she nodded after a few seconds and smiled.

"You're going to need an environmental suit. It's pretty nasty in there,"

Grayson hated it how his stomach twisted into a painful knot as he realised that things were going to get a hell of a lot worse before they could ever get better.

***

Grayson had always hated damn environmental suits. He hated their bright red appearance that made him look like a tomato, he hated how his movements were so slow and controlled and he hated how it was always just damn impossible to see out of them.

Even now as he slowly went into the environmentally sealed Ultraspace chamber, an immense black metal chamber with two huge metal tanks containing strange complex technology allowing them to tap into Ultraspace whenever they wanted, Grayson realised just how bad this all actually was.

He had been in chambers like this all over the Imperium and they never changed much but they were always clean, smelt sweet and they always left the taste of lemon drizzle cake on his tongue just like how his father used to make it when he was a child.

But this chamber was simply disgusting with the smell and taste of harsh chemicals, toxic radiation and death filling his senses. His suit's warning systems were already starting to flare to life and no one else knew this but Grayson knew there was a rip in Ultraspace.

He had read about Ultraspace rips plenty of times and they were always kept under wraps and a strange type of radiation always leaked into the ships and sometimes something worse leaked through with them.

He didn't know what the reports said about the so-called creatures that leaked through the rips but people died and then became ghosts of a fashion. Grayson had no intention of dying today so he looked around for a weapon but there weren't any.

He had thought he was going to die plenty of times in battle, on ships or getting involved in beer brawls. Normally he didn't care about dying as long as it was in service but for some reason he just felt closer to Death than even before.

As Grayson went towards the two metal tanks he could have sworn that he heard laughter and people wanting him to do something. It was like a corrupting chant in the back of his mind urging him to do something dangerous.

He felt the urge to remove his helmet so he could breathe more freely and not have to listen to the constant groan of his breathing but he couldn't.

He had to stay alive or everyone else on the ship might die too.

Grayson took out a smaller scanner that he had picked up on the way over here and he started scanning the chamber and surprisingly enough the Ultraspace Generator was working perfectly.

In fact, everything was apparently working perfectly, or it was working well enough not to register.

Grayson looked at Mary and just frowned as she had completely removed her environmental suit, her eyes had sunken in on themselves and her feet were now ghostly.

He shook his head as he realised that the rip had corrupted her and she had come to get him because he was the only one that could stop the corruption.

"Death is the ruler of the Network not humanity," Mary said. "Humanity might have wiped out my creations of the Keres but we will rise again,"

Grayson broke out into a fighting position. He had no idea what the hell had corrupted Mary but it was clearly insane.

Sure humanity wanted to obliterate the aliens but they weren't dead yet sadly. So this corrupting creature had to be something to do with their strange alien mythology and abominable magic.

This creature had to die.

The creature infecting Mary just grinned and kept looking at him up and down like he was a piece of meat ready for the slaughter.

Grayson tried to think harder about what had happened to the surviving members of the ships where rips had occurred. He couldn't remember. He knew he had to close the rip but he didn't know how.

He didn't even know how the rips occurred in the first place.

"I see your mind human. You fear me. And just know that Death grows stronger so your Network will die like your race,"

Mary charged.

Her fingers became swords.

She slashed them.

Grayson rolled to one side.

He couldn't move.

His suit wasn't flexible enough.

He was stuck.

He felt Mary slashed his back.

Grayson screamed as radiation poured into him.

His lungs roared as toxic chemicals filled them.

He screamed as his body turned cancerous.

Every single cell felt like it was fire and then his world went black.

But he knew that he had died for sure.

***

Grayson hated how ghostly, light and strange he felt as he woke up on the bright white floor of an Ultraspace Tunnel. It felt so weird to be inside a tunnel and yet not blinded by its intense white sterile light with a few white circular ships zooming overhead.

The air was unfortunately cold, icy and bitter and Grayson really didn't like how the air smelt of damp, but he just couldn't understand why he was inside a tunnel and not dead-dead.

He looked down at his legs, arms and chest and he bit his lip as he realised that he was like a ghost. He wasn't completely see-through but he might as well have been.

When he turned around Grayson shook his head as he saw a tear the size of his hand behind him, he went out to touch it but crippling pain filled him. He knew that the rip lead to his ship but he was dead so he could never return.

A strange suckling and humming and buzzing sound came from behind him.

Grayson turned around and he wanted to swear as he saw a very thin shadowy black figure like the Grim Reaper carrying his scythes that Grayson just knew was dripping his own blood.

The figure didn't smile or anything, or maybe he was because Grayson couldn't see his face but the figure was immensely tall, easily five times the height of him. And yet Grayson had no idea what he was.

"I told you I get more and more powerful each day human," the figure said.

"What are you?" Grayson asked. "I don't know you. I don't know who you are. You are nothing to me,"

Grayson guessed that made the Figure smile.

"I am one of the Gods that you claim don't exist. The Keres called me The Destroyer but I prefer the term The Obliterator. Now you have served in your military. You know what I can do?"

Grayson looked to the bright white floor for a moment and he did sort of remember the strange heretical beliefs of the Keres. They believed in a Dark and Light group of gods with The Destroyer being the creator of their Death Magic but they were just myths.

Myths created by a strange doomed dying pathetic race of aliens that humanity would hopefully slaughter one day.

The figure echoed. "Humans are so stupid. You doubt I exist but I feed on your thoughts, your dreams, your ambitions every single time you travel through my network. Do you think it was an accident that your Rex found the Network?"

Grayson nodded.

"Of course not. I grow stronger with more of my Dark Gods are being found and soon I will be free of this prison and soon the galaxy shall burn once again with my rage,"

"Again?" Grayson asked.

The Figure laughed even more. "It is amazing humans can even begin to imagine the grandeur and complexities of the galaxy but I will not tell you anymore. So how about we make a deal?"

Grayson really didn't know what to do about this figure, he was clearly evil, deranged and hellbent on destroying humanity but he could also be a weapon against the Keres. And any weapon against the Keres was a good friend to Grayson.

"Whatever you want," Grayson said.

The Figure laughed as he stretched out a palm without fingers and black energy shot out of them.

The tendrils of black magic swirled, twirled and whirled around Grayson and he screamed in agony for a brief moment as the magic turned him to ash.

But whilst he knew that humanity was ultimately doomed if they didn't learn how to work with the Keres instead of facing them because of the sheer power of the servants of The Destroyer, he knew that his life, knowledge and power was being exchanged for sealing up the rip.

So his friends, crew and ship were now safe and Grayson smiled as he finally became just another white light in the tunnels because he had done his mission, and that would have to be enough for now.

And at least he died in service. Just like he always wanted.

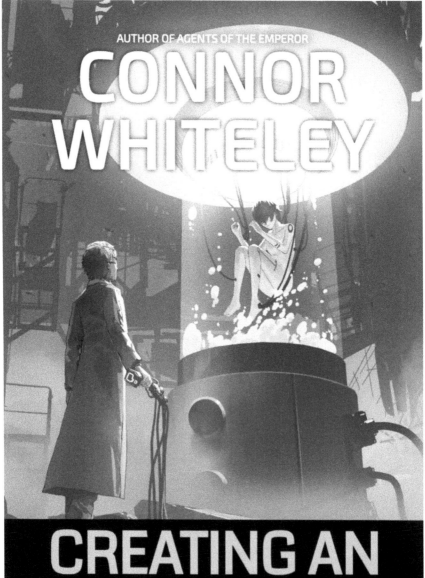

AUTHOR OF AGENTS OF THE EMPEROR

CONNOR WHITELEY

CREATING AN ARCHANGEL

A SCIENCE FICTION GENETIC ENGINEERING SHORT STORY

CREATING AN ARCHANGEL

Professor Charlotte Everlonge carefully slipped through the heavy, impossibly thick and very reinforced metal door that her Master had always warned her to avoid. She had never understood if the door was so important then why there were no signs, no markings, no nothing on the door or around it.

Considering the University De Confederate was the most famous and privileged university on Terra let alone the Confederacy, it seemed stupid to not protect the door a little better.

Charlotte carefully closed the heavy door behind her, thankful she didn't slam or smash it against the frame, and she was shocked. She was inside a huge black room, probably large enough to fit a talon-like shuttle inside like her father had ridden when it was a soldier (cannon fodder for the superhuman Angels of Death and Hope). The massive black coiled cable as thick as her arm lined the walls.

It was impressive as hell to see so many thousands upon thousands of cables probably filled with water, genetic material and even liquid food just hanging there running down the walls and floor towards something in the middle of the chamber. She used the cables every day with her students in the genetic labs, showing her brilliant students how to grow, manipulate and vat-grown an organic creature.

It was only the first term so right now, her first-year students were growing mice from raw DNA sequences, whilst her final years were growing dogs and cats from scratch. And her PhD students were growing baseline humans from DNA extracts from fallen soldiers. One day Charlotte really wanted to grow superhumans from DNA but the Confederacy had banned that, at the moment.

The entire chamber stunk of rich, buttery smoked salmon and freshly baked bread rolls with large doses of fried onions, rosemary and garlic. Charlotte licked her lips and her mouth watered at the sensational aromas. She had only ever known her Master, professor Tesserae Vain to have that combination.

Why would she be working in here?

She went deeper into the chamber, stepping over the lumpy, bumpy cables that made the air crackle, hum and pop a little. The cables moved a little under her feet as the liquid inside them gushed through them towards their target.

And then she saw the target at last.

Behind a tall row of large black computers, like the ones from ancient Earth with awfully primitive glass screens and something called a "hard drive" and monitor, she saw something she had only read about. There was an immense cylinder of bright blue glowing liquid and there was a humanoid creature floating in the liquid.

She went over to the creature. It looked just like the Angels her father had mentioned on the two liberty breaks he had been allowed home on before he was ripped to shreds by an alien disease on a long-dead world. It was easily four metres tall, arms as thick as trees and muscle perfect for ripping a monster limb from limb.

No wonder the Angels were their main line of defense against the corrupt, weak Great Human Empire and the foul aliens that preyed on the other species of the galaxy. Yet this humanoid creature seemed different too, his fingers weren't completely human, his eyes were oval and his ears were pointy.

There was something else about the creature's aura too that she just couldn't pin down. She normally hated talk of auras, energies and other mythic crap that she quickly drilled out of her students, but there was something weird about this creature.

The heavy metal door opened.

Charlotte tensed. She couldn't be caught. She couldn't be fined. She could not afford any disciplinary action to be taken against her. It would end her career as a professor and researcher and geneticist.

She rushed over to the ancient computers and ducked under the "monitor". She couldn't stop her body shaking. She could not be caught.

"Charlotte?" Tesserae asked.

Charlotte wanted to scream. She was caught, she was done for, her life was over. She saw that Tesserae was staring at the creature. What if Tesserae unleashed the creature on her?

She just watched in horror. Tesserae was actually here in her long white lab coat. She was here on business. She was here to do something. Everyone at the university knew Tesserae attacked students and even staff who stopped her working.

Had Charlotte stopped her working?

"I will not hurt you if you come out from under the computer," Tesserae said still not looking at her.

Charlotte really didn't want to come out. She knew that Tesserae was unstable, harsh and evil. Tesserae could turn on her at any moment. Her career could still be over.

After a few moments, she took a long deep breath of the delicious delightfully scented air and nodded to herself. She was a Professor just like Tesserae, she was going to be fine because she hadn't really done anything wrong. Tesserae would not hurt her and she would be fine.

Charlotte crawled out of her hiding spot and Tesserae grinned at her. The other Professor tucked a long grey curl behind her ear and gestured Charlotte to join her.

"I am glad you finally wanted to explore this space because I want you on this project with me," Tesserae said.

Charlotte forced herself to smile and nod. Like hell was she getting involved on a project with Tesserae. The woman might have been a great Master, watching over, supervising and supporting her whilst she taught students. Yet Tesserae was crazy.

"This is the project that could change the war forever," Tesserae said taking out a knife.

Charlotte did not want to die. She hated knives ever since her mother had accidentally cut her as a teenager when they were making dinner together.

Tesserae tapped the knife against the glass. The humanoid creature's eyes opened.

Charlotte wanted to step back as she saw the creature's glowing black and gold eyes twirling and staring at her. The creature couldn't have cared less about Tesserae, but Charlotte just felt uncomfortable as the creature stared at her.

"What is it?" Charlotte asked.

"Archangel," Tesserae said.

Charlotte shook her head. This was bad and she had to focus now. She had read an article years ago, hell everyone had, about a Talon of the Lord Ophelia Lockwood bringing back some creature from an Empire research base. It was meant to be a super soldier far beyond the strengths, powers and lethality of even the Angels.

How the hell that was possible was beyond Charlotte.

Yet Archangel was destroyed, the Empire had embedded a self-destruct protocol into the very DNA of the creature. It was dead. Gone. Impossible to reproduce.

"Do not tell me you are a failure too," Tesserae said pointing the blade at Charlotte's throat.

"Of course not," Charlotte said knowing what her Master was playing at. "The Lord of War probably hired hundreds, thousands, maybe even mandated every geneticist in the Confederacy to try and recreate the creature,"

Tesserae nodded and the damn creature still kept staring at Charlotte. She really wanted the creature dead.

She was almost surprised at the idea. There was something so unnatural, disturbing and gross about the sheer perfection of Archangel. She supposed she was a servant of the Lord of War so she should have been grateful for the advancement.

She couldn't be grateful. This Archangel never should have existed.

"Is he complete?" Charlotte asked as the cables under her moved and churned as more liquid was forced through them.

Archangel grinned inside the liquid as it glowed even more, probably from all the extra genetic material, nutrients and whatever other unnatural crap Tesserae was pumping into him.

"No," Tesserae said frowning and she lowered the knife. "He is stronger than any Angel judging by my computer tests but I need you. I cannot get him to breathe on his own. He has lungs but cannot use them,"

Charlotte grinned. That was a hell of a problem and at least that meant Archangel could die, if she could simply break the glass. She didn't really want to, because creating an Archangel from barely any information or research was a major feat and advancement in confederate genetics.

Yet Archangel kept staring at her and now the creature was grinning and slashing his serpentine tongue at her. She needed him to die.

"You probably messed up the genetics so they don't produce the correct surfactant proteins to keep the lungs inflated by reducing surface tension,"

Tesserae glared at her. "Are you saying *I* made a mistake? *You* are the one that publishes papers on the genetics of the respiratory system,"

Charlotte couldn't believe the arrogance of the damn woman. "Do not lecture me on my research. You know the function of the respiratory system is an interaction between the nervous system, genetics and the environment and-"

Charlotte stopped. She noticed the Archangel was grinning at her and his unnaturally talon-like fingers were pressing against the glass.

"What sort of pressure can that glass withstand?" Charlotte asked.

Tesserae went over to her computers and activated them. Charlotte saw thousands of lines of analogue code. She couldn't even understand it, it was so different from High Confederate that this was a mystery.

The glass started cracking.

The Archangel screamed bloody murder as glowing red liquid was pumped into the creature, and Charlotte felt a little sorry for him. A small part of her never wanted this creature to suffer, it was a living thing and it had never had a choice in its creation, but there was something unnatural and sickening about it.

"There," Tesserae said. "There was an error in the code about the proteins you mentioned,"

Charlotte so badly wanted to point out how it was Tesserae's line of code that had been errored, but she didn't.

Then the reality of the situation sunk in.

She felt the black cables under her feet move and alternate between being lumpy and bumpy and gross as more new nutrients and genetic material was added to the Archangel.

Charlotte had always taught her first-year students that at the University de Confederacy their technology was so advance an easy genetic change could take minutes to take effect once pumped into a creature's vat-tank.

Within minutes the Archangel would be healed enough to be able to use his own lungs and breathe oxygenated air. He wouldn't need a vat, he wouldn't need life support and he certainly wouldn't need liquid anymore.

"He's more powerful than an Angel, you say?" Charlotte asked.

Tesserae nodded. "If an Angel is worth the strength of a hundred normal baseline soldiers. Archangel can rip through a thousand soldiers before even breaking a sweat or taking damage,"

Charlotte could not allow that to happen. She hated the aliens. She hated the Empire. She hated all enemies of the Confederacy but that much power was wrong. No one deserved to have *that* much destruction in their hands.

She had to stop the Archangel.

Tesserae's knife was weakly held in her hand.

Charlotte went for it.

Tesserae whipped the knife around, grabbed Charlotte and whacked her across the face.

Charlotte flat out hated the lumpy black cables pressing against her back. It was even worse when Tesserae climbed on top of her and wrapped a loose cable round her throat.

The Archangel pressed against the cracking glass even more.

"You are *not* taking the Archangel away from me," Tesserae said pressing the knife against her throat. "This is my ticket to the halls of power. I will sit on the High Council, I will shake hands with the Lord of War and I will usher in a new age of science and power and war,"

Charlotte opened her mouth but she couldn't. She hadn't realised up until now just how much of the Confederacy was all about lies, control and oppression. She had been a history student before the Confederacy bombed her school, kidnapped her and her family and brainwashed them in the Mindcamps.

She had been taught like everyone else, the people who had been born in the Confederacy, that the Lord of War's iron grip on humanity was for the greater good. It was the Lord's total control over every single aspect of society that kept them safe.

Charlotte just looked at the knife pressed against her throat and realised it was all a lie. Tesserae was so brainwashed and believed so much in the Lord's lies that she was willing to create the ultimate monster to achieve greatness that she honestly, probably didn't even believe herself.

"I am sorry I have to kill you," Tesserae said grinning. "Not,"

Tesserae slashed Charlotte's throat.

The Archangel exploded out of the tank.

Glass shards rained down on the chamber. Slicing through the air. Slashing Tesserae's right eye.

Charlotte felt her warm blood drip onto her face as she struggled to breathe.

The genetic liquid gushed out the tank and flooded the chamber. The computer buzzed, crackled and exploded.

The Archangel flew at Tesserae.

Charlotte could only see Tesserae scream in utter terror and she could see the white of Tesserae's eyes.

In the blink of an eye Tesserae's head exploded, cracked like an egg by a single hand of the Archangel and now the immense creature stood over Charlotte.

She shook even more and gasped for breath as even more of her own dark red blood gushed out of her neck.

The Archangel stared at her for a moment and slashed his own wrists with his talon-like fingers and he poured the blood over her wound. Charlotte hissed in pain at the touch of the icy cold blood and it seeped into her wound.

The two bloods mixed and Charlotte felt sick, bile rose up in her throat as she felt their DNA mix and combine. Then she gasped as she felt the wound sew itself back together and the Archangel didn't stop pouring blood into her until she had enough to replace all the blood she lost.

Charlotte sat up and smiled weakly at the creature just as it slumped over, and Charlotte was surprised at herself. She didn't rush over, embrace and hug the creature. She simply stood up and smiled.

The Archangel smiled back at her and his eyes turned watery. Charlotte knew the creature could heal itself, it was stronger than an Angel, and they could heal from wounds that would kill mortal men with such ease it was like child's play. She didn't doubt the Archangel could do the same even quicker.

Charlotte went over to the Archangel and held its massive head in her arms.

"You want to die, don't you?" Charlotte said as the Archangel nodded. "You never had a choice in your creation and you are probably far smarter than all of us combined. You know you have too much power, you would never be free and you would never be loved,"

A single tear ran down the Archangel's cheek. Charlotte was impressed with his language comprehension but he probably couldn't speak High Confederate. Language was learnt, it wasn't genetic after all.

"I am sorry this happened to you," Charlotte said hugging him as the Archangel took his final breath.

"Thank you," he said before he died.

***

A few weeks later, Charlotte slipped past the heavy, impossibly thick and extremely reinforced door once more and nodded her *hellos* to all her final year, Masters and PhD students as they gathered in the chamber where the Archangel had died earlier.

Tesserae was officially erased from all records and Charlotte was now in charge of the genetic and biological sciences at the University de Confederacy. Something she hardly minded and she flat out loved her new job monitoring all the wonderful research, supervising the other lecturers and meeting even more great students.

The Confederacy was certainly going to enter a new golden age of science, genetics and discovery and she couldn't wait.

Charlotte went across all the lumpy, bumpy metal cables that hung down from the ceiling and ran across the floor towards the brand-new vat-tank. It was great there were so many students here all in their sterile white lab coats with golden thread running round the shoulders and seams. They were all grinning at her and she could literally feel the excitement buzzing in the air.

All because she was going to announce the Confederacy had approved her application. They were going to try vat-growing superhuman Angels of Death and Hope.

She doubted it could actually be done but it was going to be an insanely fun challenge for sure. And unlike Archangel, Angels of Death and Hope were a lot less powerful, they were loved and they were free to do as they wanted within reason.

Charlotte stood in front of a brand-new crystal clear vat-tank and grinned as the even newer bright blue holographic computers (that were so much better than the unhackable computer relics from ancient earth) activated.

"On the holograms around you are your groups for this term," Charlotte said as she started explaining how this new academic term was going to work, what their aims were and why this was so critical to the security of themselves, the Confederacy and their future.

She was largely just reading from a script given to her by a member of Confederate Government, but she didn't care. This was her project and she was going to usher in a new golden age of science, genetics and discovery all whilst carefully silencing projects that were far too dangerous.

It was why she had secretly requested permission to create a vat-grown Angel. If she failed then no one else would ever do it again because it would be deemed impossible.

And that was exactly what she intended to do. She intended to fail, learn a lot of great things along the way and prevent anyone else from creating vat-grown Angels. It was simply too dangerous and no one should have the power to engineer entire armies at the press of a keyboard and the gush of some liquid.

She was done creating monsters, soldiers and especially Archangels.

AUTHOR OF AGENTS OF THE EMPEROR SERIES

CONNOR WHITELEY

CORRUPTING DARKNESS

A SCIENCE FICTION FAR FUTURE SHORT STORY

CORRUPTING DARKNESS

Thick choking aromas of smoke, charred flesh and boiling blood filled Captain Henry Oblong's senses as his eyes slowly flickered open. He had no idea where he was, how he had gotten here or what was actually happening.

All he could do was focus on the terrible, ugly, awful smell that seemed to fill the air like the evil cousin of oxygen was trying to replace it. Henry coughed and he just wanted to be okay. He hated the foul taste of charred flesh that formed on his tongue.

Henry didn't want to be on some strange alien world. He wanted to be protecting humanity, saving people's lives and just helping to make sure humanity lasted one day at a time in this cold deadly galaxy.

He slowly tried to move his hands side to side to feel what he was on or at least touching, he was surprised by the sheer icy coldness of the sandy ground beneath him. He realised he was on his back, winded and he was struggling to breathe.

Henry really tried to remember why the hell he was here. He was an Imperial soldier he knew that, he had enlisted when he was 16 to make sure that humanity was protected against the traitors, aliens and the so-called magic that certain alien races were corrupted by.

Henry had no idea at all why he was on his back on a planet filled with such an awful atmosphere. It was so disgusting that he actually wanted to be sick but real soldiers do not vomit. That was the golden rule of the Imperium.

After a few more seconds of choking and struggling to breathe, Henry forced himself up and he really focused on his surroundings.

He was surprised that there was nothing around him except the burning, crackling and popping wreckage of bright a white pod that he had been travelling in. Henry was meant to meet up with a massive Imperial fleet that was gathering in the area to scourge the aliens off these worlds.

As much as Henry wanted to go over to the pod, he sadly knew there was nothing he could do now. The pod was destroyed and Henry guessed it was hardly natural for an Imperial pod to get blown out the sky. It was probably shot, bombed or maybe some foul magic had forced it to land.

Henry hated aliens and he was going to kill them all in the end.

Henry forced his attention away from the pod and hated the sheer thickness of the black smoke that swirled, twirled and whirled around him. It didn't seem natural because there wasn't any wind, there were no forces at play here to explain what he was seeing and Henry didn't like how he felt like he was being watched.

The coldness of the air made him shiver and Henry realised that unless he made it to shelter or something soon. He was going to die and then humanity had one less soldier to defend itself with. Something he absolutely couldn't allow.

Henry forced himself to take a step forward then another then another.

Henry felt like he was swimming through pea soup or something just as harsh, cold and evil. He had thankfully heard and studied and killed more magical aliens, Keres, than he cared to think about but this wasn't their style.

The Keres were a dying out alien race that were weak, pathetic and evil down to their very core. Yet their pathetic-ness made them cowards at heart so they were all about ambushing and this wasn't ambushing.

Henry could have sworn he saw shadows and figures move in the darkness of the smoke but as soon as he blinked they were gone.

The smoke burnt his eyes and caused water to stream down his face this was a nightmare and he hated every single minute of it.

He felt around for his gun, knife and pistol that he always carried on his waist but they were gone. Henry swore under his breath as he forced himself to continue.

If the enemy had shot him down then there was no telling what he was dealing with so the only ally he had here was higher ground so he could hopefully get out of this damn smoke.

Then he took a step that changed everything.

Henry stepped forward and jerked himself as he no longer felt sand under his feet but something hard and shiny and awful as he found himself in a brand-new black crystal chamber.

He had no clue what had just happened but this was bad. The chamber was large made from shiny black crystal that pulsed with blood red energy and Henry felt like he was meant to touch it.

He knew that would be a bad idea if there ever was one.

The air stunk of charred flesh, ash and death as Henry paced around hoping for a way out of the chamber but there wasn't one.

The domed ceiling made from shiny black crystal was even brighter with blood red energy than the sides, and Henry really wanted to escape.

The crystal walls of the prison hummed, vibrated and banged. Henry broke into a fighting stance and then he swore the foul aliens that he had never thought he would see behind this most unholy act against humanity.

Out of the crystal walls a single very tall and scarily thin humanoid female stepped out. Blood red energy glowed on her pale white skin and face and body where veins and arties should have been.

Henry just focused on the female's pointy, sharp face that he was fairly sure could be used as a weapon in its own right. She was a Keres but definitely not one of the aliens he had seen before.

The female swirled her hand and red magical energy made the air crackle as she smiled.

"Captain Henry," the female said, her human tongue harsh, unrefined and just plain awful.

Henry wanted to kill her there and then. All the foul Keres knew that under the Treaty of Defeat attacking humanity was the worst possible crime, punishable by extermination.

Of course humanity was allowed to kill the Keres as they pleased but if the Keres were less bestial then they might have won the war instead of being defeated like the pathetic creatures they were.

"I was excited to meet such a kill like yourself," the female said her voice becoming more and more of an echo. "I had wondered by the glory of Geneitor would make our paths cross,"

Henry just rolled his eyes. It was beyond pathetic of the Keres to believe in their flawed and unholy mythology about how a God called Geneitor had created death and sought to kill all life but the Mother of Creation Genetrix sought to protect it.

"Release me demon," Henry said. "Your race is breaking the law and I will burn you for it,"

The female smiled. "Then my species does not have much of an incentive to do that, does it? And I have much more important uses for you in the services of Geneitor,"

"I will never turn, I will never reveal secrets and I will always protect humanity,"

The female laughed. "Every single human says that when I capture them but they always turn,"

"I am not a normal human," Henry said. "I am a soldier, a hero of humanity and I am a killer of the Keres,"

The female shivered in pleasure and Henry wanted to be sick.

"His Lordship is grateful for the souls of the murdered so thank you. They keep him powerful, stirring and strong enough to one day return to this dying galaxy so he can complete what the foul Mother stopped him from doing," she said.

Henry shook his head.

He charged.

The female clicked her fingers and Henry froze. He tried to

fight, scream, kick. He couldn't do anything.

"Humans are always so inelegant and you haven't asked me who I am," the female said. "My name is The Corrupter, a champion of Geneitor and it is my job to corrupt the souls of Keres and humans alike so they may serve him even in death,"

Henry laughed. He had never heard of such rubbish in all his life.

"Let us take a little trip around my encampment,"

Before Henry could ever think about protesting, choking blood red smoke engulfed him and he felt the world fall away from him.

***

Henry was hardly impressed with the stupid Corrupter as he found himself alone standing in the middle of a massive group of skin-crafted tents with a roaring, crackling fire in the middle.

He had to admit that tents were domed, ugly and Henry realised he didn't need to have magic to know that they were crafted out of human skin, there was even some blood and muscle still attached to some sheets of skin flapping about in the coldness of the air.

He enjoyed the scents of flowers, jasmine and chilli in the air before it was leaving replaced with the foul scent of charred flesh that was so strong in the air he was almost choking. He hated the Keres.

The flames of the fire danced a little and a moment later the Corrupter appeared smiling at him in fiery form.

"It is amazing that you believe we are Keres, but we are Dark Keres, Fallen Keres or Shadow Walkers depending on what idiots you ask about us," the Corrupter said.

"Why bring me here? Why not just kill me and let your false God feast on my soul?" Henry asked knowing that Geneitor was nothing more than a myth created by a dying alien race.

The Corrupter laughed. "Look around you Captain Henry,"

Henry nodded as he stared at the skin-crafted tents and how cold, unloved and isolated each of them looked. Then he saw long feral claws were reaching out of the tents.

"This is what I have had to do to save Keres race. Souls keep

Geneitor alive long enough for his influence to spread but the Great War must be fought and the Keres race must be saved,"

"What are you talking about? Your race is an abomination that deserves to die," Henry said.

Henry walked round to the other side of the fire and he was surprised that not a single hint of warmth came from it.

"When humanity attacked my home planet, burnt my village, killed my entire family. I escaped into the Ultraspace network, you know that intergalactic transport system you stole from us,"

Henry smiled. That was definitely one of the greatest benefits of the war and it was so worth all the bloodshed that righteous humanity had committed.

"I was about to die in the network when Geneitor found me, he convinced me to serve him and he shared some of his power with me. He gave me the secret to destroying humanity and saving the Keres race,"

Henry shook his head. These aliens deserved to die and there was nothing she could say that would convince him otherwise.

"I need to find the Stones of Geneitor and bring him into this universe so we can wipe out humanity once and for all. Then my race can be safe again with the God of Death looking over us,"

Henry spat at her. "If your God is so powerful then why can my species kill you all so easily,"

"The Dark Keres are outcasts, hunted by the mainstream Keres in case humanity learn about us and wage war against us once more. The Keres are scared and look at what the Dark Keres have been reduced to,"

Henry didn't care that these aliens had been reduced to living out of skin-crafted tents, forced to eat corpse meat off the bone judging by the bones littering the campsite, and he really didn't care the Dark Keres were weak.

"You are a dying race and that is it," Henry said. "You cannot make anything, you cannot protect yourself, you cannot do anything,"

The Corrupter sighed. "That is all true and we have no need for money or trade because the gifts of the Destroyer but I was hoping to turn you more easily but watch what I show you next. This is the truth,"

Henry was about to protest when his mind started to fill with images of dying humans, men and women just being murdered by other humans. There were images of corruption and evil bargains being struck in the highest levels of Imperial Government and more images revealed the creation of super weapons.

Henry knew they were being created to be used against the Enlightened Republic, the stupid breakaway regions of humanity that believed in democracy against the righteous control of the Rex.

So many innocent humans would be destroyed simply because they chose democracy over the Rex. That was wrong and Henry didn't want that.

The people of the Enlightened Republic needed to be sent to re-education camps not killed.

"Geneitor could save them all," The Corrupter said. "You once mentioned to a friend that your purpose is to save humanity, protect it and keep innocent people alive,"

Henry nodded that was the entire point of his being.

"If you join Geneitor I can promise you that these people will be saved, protected and live alongside the Keres. The Republic has no problem with my race so they will not be killed,"

Henry had to agree with her there. He knew the Imperium would wipe out all non-Imperial fractions sooner or later that meant a lot of innocent people dying.

Henry looked at the Corrupter. "Are there such things as innocent Keres?"

The Corrupter stepped out of fire returning to her flesh and blood form. Her pale white face smiling at him.

"Me and Geneitor can promise you that the Keres did not start this war. Humanity was scared of our power and that made them shoot first,"

Henry felt something start to press against his mind. It felt so pleasurable, calming and safe like it was a parent offering him a hug, maybe the Keres were not so bad after all and if humanity was capable of so much murder and bloodshed then maybe they did need to be stopped with Genitor's help.

That way he could continue to help humanity, save lives and just protect every single human he had always wanted to do ever since he was 16 years old.

"What will happen to me when I convert?" Henry asked.

The Corrupter smiled and hugged him. "Nothing bad. You will simply accept Geneitor into your heart, mind and body. You will become stronger, tougher and see the universe in a brand-new way,"

Henry nodded. It sounded scary as hell but he had to protect humanity no matter the cost.

"But I will warn you if you choose this path then humanity will hunt you down, mainstream Keres will hunt you down and so will the Daughters of Generatrix. Is that a risk you would want to take?"

Henry nodded.

The Corrupter smiled and Henry's mind exploded as he became a Dark Keres.

***

Six months later, Henry smiled as he stood on a massive desert planet covered in golden sand for as far as the eye could see. There were no dunes, no hills nor mountains but Henry was more than glad about that. It meant there were basically no places for the evil humans to run away to.

The air stunk of jasmine, flowers and mint that left the great taste of mint ice cream form on his tongue. He had no idea why the humans had choked and coughed and hissed in pain as they breathed in the air but that was the stupid thing about humans they just didn't know what was good for them.

Henry gripped his bone spear tightly as his fellow Keres came over to him. They all looked so great, angelic and beautiful with their long claws, bone spikes shooting out of their armour and their long fangs looked perfect as they dripped small amounts of blood onto the ground.

Henry still couldn't believe it had taken so long for him to accept Genitor's gifts because that was the thing about the Destroyer, he was never a bad man, he didn't destroy people's minds. He only gave them the tools to realise that the galaxy was an evil place and humanity was the greatest challenge they faced.

Humanity had to die to make sure the Keres survived and that was all that mattered.

Henry licked his fangs with his hard snake tongue as he looked forward to hunting down the rest of the humans on the planet and sacrifice their fat juicy souls to Genitor and hopefully some of them would even see the enlightenment that the Destroyer had offered him.

Humanity was going to pay for their sin of existence and Henry had no problem with that at all.

It was going to be a beautifully dark and bloody future, exactly what the God of Death wanted and Henry didn't want to disappoint his Lord and Master. Not for a single second.

CONNOR WHITELEY

BLACKHEART

A SCIENCE FICTION FAR FUTURE SHORT STORY

BLACKHEART

Brother meets brother.

Being Imperial Regent has a hell of a lot of great, amazing and rather delightful benefits that I, Jack Blackheart, certainly enjoy most of the time. Especially, as I stood on the very top of the immense black metal Imperial Fortress with the icy cold wing slowly rubbing my cheeks dry.

I had always enjoyed the Fortress way too much actually. It was such a beacon of the Rex's immense power, authority and sheer brutality with its huge black 8-point star design that stretched on for thousands of miles in all directions and upwards even more.

It was next to impossible to look down below and see the charred black stone ground that so many soldiers walked over every day, because it was their duty to the Rex. I actually wanted to know if they did this out of choice but I doubted I could ever get a reliable answer.

The part of the fortress I was standing on had to be my favourite. I was north towards the largest city on Earth and it might have been miles upon miles away but it still looked great with its fiery spires reaching up into space and so many little beautiful lights of ships, shuttles and fighters buzzing around the city like bees.

The wind might have been icy cold scented with wonderful hints of jasmine, lavender and peanuts leaving the good taste of nature on my tongue but I honestly could have stayed out here for hours.

And that city was so damn beautiful.

On cold dark nights like this, it was something to behold and it just reminded me how great humanity could be. When I first joined the Rex, I was so filled with hope about the Imperium.

Of course back then I believe, I believed the Imperium was a force for good, change and the betterment of everyone. But that was a lie, probably the biggest lie in human history because the Imperium was all about control these days.

I was probably the most free person in the Imperium because I was the Rex's right and left hand but even I felt the imposing stare of security cameras from time to time. So I just admired the sheer beauty of the nearby city and just dreamed for a single moment that the people in the city might be free, laughing and smiling with each other.

Footsteps came up behind me and I dared to imagine it was someone to save me.

I just had to smile at that idea because whenever I visited a place in the Imperium, I always donated Rexes, food and machinery to the local population just so they might have a better life, and maybe I could continue to believe in that small, small moment that the Imperium was a force for good once again.

I often argued with myself about leaving, running away and just abandoning the Rex to his crazy delusions of control and power but I didn't want to.

As stupid as it sounded this was still my home, the Rex had found me when I was a late teenager on the streets and starving so he bought me in, gave me food and shelter.

And I served him, happily at first and now I just press on because the work can be great at times.

"You're up late tonight, Lord Regent,"

I recognised the voice instantly. It was a deep female voice so I turned around and grinned at my old friend Perrigin, or Perry for short, in a great-looking blue dress, military boots and small gun in her hand. She still looked beautiful.

She was meant to be in charge of forcing the various Planetary

Governors in the Imperium to the Rex's Will but she was so good at it that most of them didn't notice they were being manipulated. And most of the time Perry was just too much fun to be around.

But she looked serious tonight.

"I never knew you had a brother," Perry said not daring to look at me.

I frowned at her. I hadn't even thought of my brother for four decades, he had abandoned me when the Rex's forces invaded our settlement and killed our parents. It was the reason why I was on the streets and it was awful.

My brother had been a good man, a hard worker and a good fighter but whilst all the other men and women in our settlement rushed to fight the invaders. My brother ran. I screamed out his name. He ran even faster.

"Why?" I asked.

Perry shrugged. "I have a new prisoner to enjoy and he claims to be your brother,"

I had to nod at that. It was a hell of a story and I still didn't understand why the Rex "gifted" prisoners to Perry. I know that her mother was an expert interrogator but I doubted she had passed on the knowledge to Perry.

"You want me to talk to him then?" I asked, really hoping she would say no so I could continue to enjoy the view.

"Yes because if this is your brother then I want to know why he was sneaking about trying to assassinate the Rex," Perry said frowning.

A lump caught in my throat as I realised that if this was truly my brother then he was a dead man. As much as I too wanted the Rex dead, I certainly wasn't stupid enough to try.

He was too smart, too well protected and too damn paranoid to ever allow an assassin within two miles of him. Let alone allow an assassin into his Fortress.

"Take me to him," I said.

Perry hugged me, grabbed me by the hand and she dragged me

towards the prisoner.

This wasn't going to end well I knew that for sure.

***

One of the many foundational lies the Imperium is built on is that the Imperium is a type of democracy where the millions upon millions of planetary governors vote amongst themselves for who should have critical roles. Like the people in charge of the military, policing, security and so on.

It's all a lie because the Rex controls everything and every single bit of freedom a person believes they have is a carefully crafted lie by the Rex himself.

I was starting to understand that now.

I followed Perry into a massive stone domed chamber with rough grey walls and it was barely large enough to swing a cat inside, and as soon as I stepped inside the temperature dropped so much my breath formed thick columns of vapour.

It was a horrible feeling seeing the hairs on my arms shoot up like defences and small crystals of ice formed on me. The chamber looked like it was meant to be warm and cosy but nothing could be further from the truth.

There were no white-armoured guards or soldiers in the chamber like I had seen in their thousands all over the Fortress. There was only a single man in the chamber with his cheeks and eyes swollen so much that I couldn't tell if this was my brother or not.

Sure the man had the same long raven black hair as my brother but it was burnt and ripped out in places, probably thanks to Perry.

The man's fingers were bleeding and shooting off in weird angles and I really didn't care to look at the rest of him.

I didn't have a cast-iron stomach like Perry clearly did.

My stomach twisted into a painful knot just looking at him so I focused on a small chipped spot on the domed wall behind him instead.

"You came then," he said in a course loving voice that my brother always used on me because he really did love me back in the day.

The lump from earlier returned stronger to my throat. I just couldn't believe this was my brother. The big brother that had taught me how to hack into a holo-system. The big brother that had cooked my dinners when our parents had to work late. The big brother that had loved me every moment of every day.

He was here and he was suffering.

"I came because it is my duty to the Rex," I said out of instinct.

My brother grinned. "Do you remember my name brother?"

I nodded. "Jason,"

Perry smiled as she took out a massive dagger. "This dagger is way too clean for my liking so please tell me, who are you working for?"

I forced myself not to look in horror at my friend. She shouldn't be doing this, this was wrong on so many levels.

"I would rather die than tell you Rex scum," Jason said.

Perry laughed. She went to thrust the dagger into him but I grabbed her wrist.

Her eyes widened as we both realised what the hell I had just done and I seriously hoped that Perry was going to break her orders and training by not killing me immediately.

"I will get the information from him," I said hoping to buy myself some time. "If he still doesn't give me the information then you can flay him alive if you care,"

I didn't want that to happen but I wanted more time.

Perry nodded so I went down and knelt in front of my brother's twisted tortured form.

"Did you ever find a boyfriend?" I asked smiling. That was actually what I hoped had happened to him over the years, I hoped my big brother had found love, happiness and joy.

He frowned and looked at Perry. "She killed him two years ago,"

I nodded. "I'm sorry,"

At least that ruled out any romantic links being the people helping him but I didn't know what I was hoping to achieve by getting the information from him.

He was going to die unless I could magically come up with an idea to save the both of us. I was clever. I just doubted I was that clever.

"I won't tell you who's helping me," Jason said.

"But they'll kill you if you don't,"

"They're going to kill me anyway," he said and I knew he was lying.

"Then I can promise you they'll kill you faster and less painfully," I said looking at Perry.

She rolled her eyes like I had just taken the fun out of her playtime but she nodded.

I was about to take Jason's hands but then I realised how mutilated they were and how tortured the rest of his body was. I didn't dare touch him in case it caused him crippling pain.

"Please. You protected me a lot during school and my childhood. Let me repay the favour by helping you now," I said.

He shook his head. "Why do you work for them?"

And before I realised it I was replying out of instinct. "Because the Rex is the only one that can help humanity not descend into chaos, hatred and anarchy. He is the difference between freedom and chaos and control and safety,"

Jason laughed. "I will not tell you who helped me because there was no one. I don't work with the Keres and their magic, I don't work with the Enlightened Republic and I don't work with anyone else,"

I almost believed him because humanity hated the foul alien Keres with their freakish magic with a passion. I had met people from the independent and so-called free people of the Enlightened Republic and my brother didn't have the arrogance of them, but my brother had lied.

He had admitted he worked with people because Perry had killed his boyfriend two years ago.

"You worked with your boyfriend so who are you working

with?" I asked. "I am Imperial Regent, I designed and reviewed the security plans of this Fortress myself almost daily. Unless you had inside help, it is impossible for you to do this,"

Then I looked at Perry and I frowned.

I reached for a weapon I normally carried but I was having it cleaned tonight as I was meeting the Rex tomorrow.

When I looked at Perry again she had a dagger pointed at me and I just shook my head. She was a traitorous bastard and then she clicked her fingers.

Jason screamed in agony as his bones, muscles and skin were ripped apart and reforged into the image of Jason's real form. He was tall, muscular and attractive like a university jock that all the girls gushed over. He looked perfect.

But I just couldn't believe that Perry had magic or something. I knew as Imperial Regent that it was a lie that no human could produce magic but the numbers were like 1 in every one trillion.

I had no idea that Perry had magic before now.

"So why this?" I asked.

"Because I knew you were a fake," Jason said. "My brother was a good man, he hated the Rex and he never would have attacked a woman trying to help me kill him. You have changed. You are one of his puppets,"

I shook my head and noticed there was a small red flashing light behind them and I sort of felt like I needed to make them confess.

It was a strange sensation but as soon as I thought about it I realised I was right. Yet if there was help coming to stop these assassins then I just wanted to make sure I didn't die in the process.

And the Rex's help was always conditional on me being loyal to him. If I showed any sign of weakness here then he would allow these two to kill me.

Before killing them himself.

"This isn't delusion Jason. This is just the truth. The truth is the Rex is the only person who could save humanity and that's a good person," I said not even forcing out the words.

Jason took a dagger out from his back. "I'm disappointed that you allowed yourself to believe in these lies,"

I shook my head. I had to find out what their plan was.

"And why you Perry?" I asked. "You were always good to the Rex and he rewarded you,"

"Because everything is a lie and everything will burn!" Perry shouted.

She charged at me.

I jumped back.

She swung again.

I punched her.

Jason tackled me.

Pinning me against the wall.

He whacked me round the face.

Forcing his blade against my throat.

"Why do this?" I asked. "What do you intend to achieve? Make us a democratic republic?"

"I would never allow us to become like the Enlightened Republic but Truth must happen," Perry said.

And then I realised exactly what had happened to her. My good friend Perry had simply allowed herself to think too much about reality, she questioned all the lies and propaganda and the foundations the Imperium was built on.

As Imperial Regent I often created the foundational lies and considered them, it was possible to know what was fact and what was fiction these days but reality was a lie.

Of course over the years it had destroyed my mental health, I had been on the brink so many times of just wanting to annihilate it all because I just wanted the truth.

I had never jumped off the edge. Clearly Perry had.

I looked my brother dead in the eye. He didn't want to do this. He looked vulnerable.

I punched him.

He fell backwards.

I jumped forward.

Grabbing the dagger.

Snatching it out of his hand.

He charged at me.

I thrusted the blade into his chest.

Perry charged at me.

Screaming in emotional agony.

She wasn't focusing.

She swung her blade.

I ducked.

She rushed past me.

I leapt up.

Stabbing her in the back.

And as the Rex's personal white-armoured bodyguards stormed in, I just shook my head as I stared at the corpse of my dear big brother and I truly realised that these two were always going to die tonight.

Because every single freedom a person thought they had was a simple lie created by the Rex.

This was all a test and one I feared for my life that I had passed. I hoped.

***

The next morning I was standing at my most favourite spot on the immense stone fortress walls staring at the beautiful city in the distance. The bright morning was surprisingly warm, calm and the sun was strongly beaming down on me like a spotlight. The air was wonderfully fresh with hints of jasmine, lavender and pecans filling the air and I was so glad to be alive.

Last night might as well have been a blur for all the good that happened to me. The bodyguards had stormed in and chopped up the corpses to make sure my dear brother and Perry were well and truly dead and then the chunks were taken away.

I was left alone in the room for a few moments before I confidently walked out and I almost jumped out of my own skin at the imposing sight of the Rex in his jet-black, twisted, terrifying armour.

He didn't say anything to me. He only grinned, smiled and nodded like he had been proven right about me and maybe he had.

I had always believed that I was different to the rest of the Fortress, I believed that I was playing a long game against the Rex but maybe I wasn't anything that I thought I was. Maybe I really had become the lies, deceit and carefully crafted mould of what I was meant to be by the Rex's design.

And now I was thinking about it, maybe that wasn't a bad thing. Sure the Rex was a master of manipulation but he trusted me, wanted me to live and I was already the second most powerful person in the entire Imperium so maybe, just maybe I should start acting like it.

Of course I wouldn't take the galaxy for myself but maybe I could have all the power I desired and I could become something, someone completely different to the little boy who had lost his brother and parents.

Maybe I could become something far greater but simply allowing the Rex to remain in power for a little while longer, because there was a simple truth that everyone, even people as *smart* as the Rex, forgets and that is that every ruler falls in the end.

Every King, Emperor and Regent in human history has fallen at some point and when one of them falls there is something, someone to replace them.

And I'm fully determined to make sure when the Rex falls that I am the person to replace him and history will remember my name and there is a single word that will echo across the centuries as the person who took over the Imperium after the evil Rex had fallen.

I just smiled and allowed the warm sun to embrace me lovingly as I realised just how great the future could be, and I was really looking forward to how everyone would remember the simple name *Blackheart* in the bitter end.

SUPERHEROES AND ALIENS

Today I was a sex therapist to an alien.

Now as a superhero Psychologist, I supposed I should have sort of believed in aliens for the most part because aliens were just as likely as superheroes to exist, and I existed so I have no idea why I refused to believe that aliens could ever be real.

Ever since I was a child in the early 1900s I flat out refused to believe in magic, superheroes and aliens. Granted no one believed in that rubbish back in the day because it went against God, the Church and all the other crap that people in the 1900s believed. But now that I'm a superhero I suppose I seriously should have been open to the idea.

But as I stood in my best friend's large, bright white spacious office and stared into the dark black eyes of an alien I still couldn't believe it.

I have to admit that I'm very stubborn when I want to be and I had to believe that this was a trick. The alien, after all, was a small black cube creature with shiny smooth skin, three large black eyes with a ring of glowing white around them and his (or her?) wafer-thin mouth grinned at me as I stared.

The cube couldn't hide in such an office because the office was so white, spacious and homey that the black cube of an alien just stuck out like a sore thumb. Actually it stood out like a broken thumb in a field of sheep.

That was exactly how stark the contrast was.

And it was strange how the alien gave off a strong aroma of freshly fried, crispy fish that left the great taste of salty fish and chips on my tongue. I was definitely going to have to go to the fish and chip shop on the corner afterwards.

I looked at my best friend Jack and he looked hot as always in his smart black trousers, white crisp shirt and his handsome face looked stunning in the light. His boyfriend Aiden was working in the other office between mine and Jack's and he clearly had no idea we had an alien in our practice.

And I should probably clarify that I'm Matilda Plum a superhero in the Psychology, Counselling and Therapy sector of the world. And normally I help look after people's mental health, solve their mental health difficulties and practice psychotherapy in my office.

I don't deal with aliens.

"Do you, like um, have a name?" I asked.

The alien then made a very low-pitched sound that I was fairly sure was just a sound but judging by the look on Jack's face it was something. It was actually a language that he understood.

I knew that Jack and Aiden had been spending a lot of time lately with our boss Natalia learning about the history of the Gods and superheroes and all the shenanigans that go on behind the scenes. But aliens, seriously? That was a new one.

"She doesn't understand your most honour language High One," Jack said.

Thankfully now that I knew for sure it was a language my superpowers kicked in, because my superpowers are all the myths and misconceptions surrounding psychologists so someone only has to talk to me for me to read their mind.

But as my superpowers started reading the alien's mind out of instinct, I instantly shut it down. I couldn't understand an alien's mind.

Then the black cube smiled at me again. "I am an alien from the Galactic North called a High Being. Me and my race travel world to world in search of knowledge and I believe you can help me Matilda

Plum,"

I had no idea what the strange alien was talking about but I couldn't deny I was a little intrigued.

"I've been experiencing... urges your culture would say. I've been wanting to kill my girlfriend when she approaches a certain topic and I did hit her once,"

I instantly started to listen because I was shocked that an alien wanted two mere human superheroes to try to treat his mental health difficulties.

I mean I was damn good at my job but actually helping an alien, that was a stretch. I didn't even know the first thing about alien culture, mental health and how they think.

Jack shrugged at me so I knew he wanted me to take the lead.

"What topic do you react in this way to?" I asked.

The cube looked at Jack and the two of them had a quick conversation in the low-pitched noises of the alien's language. That was just amazingly disturbing to watch.

"Sex," the alien said.

Oh wow. I had to be a sex therapist to an alien. That was so going on my CV later on, if superheroes had CVs of course.

"What makes you want to kill her?" Jack asked, even I was impressed with how non-judgemental his voice was.

I had no idea how this alien had sex let alone how to help him get some.

The alien looked a little unsure of himself so I gestured over to Jack's impressive array of bean bags, wooden chairs and sofas and the three of us went over to them.

A lot of clients think this is some psycho test but it seriously isn't. At my practice we just believe everyone should sit in whatever they want. And this is so much better when we deal with children. Children don't want to talk to us on sofas, they want to talk to us on bean bags.

The black cube alien looked unsure of himself as he sat on a light blue sofa and me and Jack sat opposite him. And I sent him some of my Trusting and Relaxing Superpowers so he would open up a little.

The alien grinned. "That superpowers feels nice. Thanks, but my problem is I cannot get my suction devices working,"

Wow. It turned out this alien race did have sex differently to humans. I was half tempted to ask him why didn't he seek professional help in his own culture but I had a feeling that this was a personal matter.

And as long as he was willing to pay I was happy and I did love helping people after all.

"The High Ones have sex by the men and women placing each other's suction devices over the top of each other. Then each one turns on their suction devices as hard as they can and whoever sucks out the liquid first gets pregnant," Jack said.

I couldn't exactly see the downside here because at least he didn't have to get pregnant. Which I have to admit is still a major concern of mine as a superhero.

"But I so badly want to get pregnant. In our culture whoever has children increases in social status, power and influence. Some parents can even fly and teleport,"

I didn't have the heart to tell the alien that I could teleport and I didn't have children, but I was human after all. I felt sorry for the alien. He clearly wanted to have children, be a father and have all these extra powers. He just didn't know how to get there.

Then I remembered something I really liked about humans.

"Friends with benefits," I said and Jack gasped and placed a firm hand over his mouth.

If the alien had a separate head from his cube I think he would have cocked his head at me.

"What's that?" he asked.

Wow. Right I had to explain friends with benefits to an alien.

"Some humans who want sex without getting into a relationship ask their friends to have sex with them so we all get what we want," I said completely unashamed that I did this at least three times a week with over superheroes. We all needed release.

The cube alien simply hopped on and down on the sofas like he was nodding or trying to think about this.

Jack smiled at me. "High Ones believe that sex is the most sacred act of all and all High Ones only have *true* sex once in their life. The rest are simply practice sessions,"

That was actually really interesting. I couldn't imagine only having sex once in my life and a few training sessions. I seriously couldn't.

"That's my problem. I'm due to have sex in two hours and I've used up all my training sessions and my suction devices still aren't strong enough for the Act," the alien said.

I stood up and paced around for a moment. I brushed my fingers over the soft warm fabric of Jack's other sofas and I had to admit that I loved a challenge.

We only had two hours to help the poor soul solve this problem or he was never going to have the chance to become a father.

The alien hopped off the sofa and also started pacing.

"Is there a way for you to get enhancements to artificially make your suction devices stronger?" I asked.

The alien shook his head. "That's illegal to High Ones. Only inferior races have enhancements,"

I so badly wanted to tell him that I see plenty of people a week with implants and that's nothing inferior about some of those boobs I see. But I could see this point.

"So you cannot delay the Act," I said. "You cannot get enhancements and you cannot what if you change your sex partner?"

The alien and Jack went silent.

"I presume if you're going to have sex in two hours you know who with," I said.

The alien shook his head. "The High One Council assigns sexual partners based on what society needs. We can make a sexual request for a certain partner but I rejected the idea. My purpose is to serve the species but my suction devices,"

This guy just doesn't make it easy on himself.

"Send another sexual request," I said. "If you really want to help your species then you becoming a father is a great way to do it. There must have been a girl or guy you wanted to have sex with in the past,"

The alien nodded in a strange alien way. "Of course. There was a girl back in my school I longed for but she's an outcast in High One because her suction devices are broken,"

I clicked my fingers. "Submit a request to have sex with her,"

Jack nodded like it was actually a good idea. I partly hated myself. I felt like it was hooking up aliens for no reason and I didn't know if the girl was even willing first of all.

"Just please tell me that the girl would want to have sex with you," I said firmly.

"How do you think we discovered her suction devices were broken?" the alien asked like it was a truly stupid question. "We were booked for a training session at age 18 and we discovered nothing worked on her,"

"My actual question," I said.

The alien nodded. "Oh yes she will definitely be willing. We always wanted to date as kids but High One culture is clear. People with faulty Suction Devices are doomed to die alone,"

That was messed up but we had our solution and I just grinned. "You need to go and make that sexual request,"

The alien grinned, laughed and made a hell of a lot of strange low-pitched noises that made him blush and then the alien flew away in a puff of black smoke.

And I just looked at Jack and laughed. If I didn't have a client with severe depression in ten minutes I would so have a drink but my work never stopped and I loved it.

***

A few hours later just before 6 pm and me, Jack and Aiden were about to head home after a large team meeting about our current clients, a loud bang came from outside and as Jack and Aiden sat up and stopped hugging each other, the door opened.

The alien rolled back into Jack's office where we were all sitting on some bean bags and he definitely had some great sex by the look on his face. And he smelt different too, he smelt like freshly roasted lamb that left the great taste of Sunday roasts on my tongue.

"Thank you darlings," he shouted like he was some dumb loved-up teenager. "I never knew sex could be so amazing and my girlfriend was sensational. I'm pregnant and now I get to have children. Thank you,"

Aiden just looked at me and Jack and I realised we definitely had some explaining to do, but we all laughed.

Then the alien disappeared again and me and Jack and Aiden just sat in silence for a minute until I smiled at my two best friends.

"Come on Aiden, let me take you out for dinner and me and Jack can explain how we were sex therapists to an alien today,"

Then the three of us skipped, laughed and snorted our way out of the building towards the local fish and chip shop. My job might have been weird, crazy and flat out mind-bending at times. But by the Gods did I love my job.

And come on, who can say they were a sex therapist to an alien? I certainly can now.

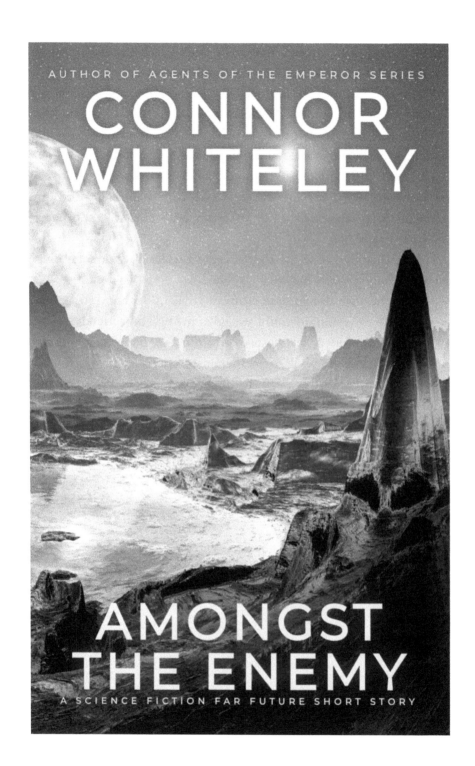

AUTHOR OF AGENTS OF THE EMPEROR SERIES

CONNOR WHITELEY

AMONGST THE ENEMY

A SCIENCE FICTION FAR FUTURE SHORT STORY

AMONGST THE ENEMY

This was the day I died.

I, Intelligence Officer Isaac Oldman, sat in the middle of an icy cold purple prison cell made from pure crystal. The prison cell wasn't too ugly, in fact it definitely had a certain beauty about it that I was shocked about.

I really enjoyed watching little creatures or whatever the foul alien Keres put into their magic crystals, as they pulsed, swirled and twirled around inside the stunning crystal. It was rather hypnotic in a strange way.

The prison cell itself wasn't much bigger than me but that was the strange thing about Keres technology, it very much had an evil mind of its own. If I wanted to stand up, the prison cell would get larger, if I wanted to sit down the entire cell would get a hell of a lot smaller. It was creepy that way and the sheer darkness of the purple crystal didn't allow me to see anything outside.

Thankfully I was an intelligence officer from the Imperial Secret Service so I was used to travelling beyond the holy realm of the Imperium and traveling into the darkness and coldness and foulness of the galaxy outside. It was only two years ago I was inside the so-called Enlightened Republic, the foul breakaway regions that were building nuclear weapons to destroy the Imperium once and for all.

All whilst they pretended to build a traitorous democracy. As if humans could actually rule themselves without the Rex's guiding light. It was just laughable.

But I knew how the foul Keres worked so I was probably stuck on some Rex-forsaken moon with thousands of other prisoners. Yet unlike me those other prisoners were probably not righteous, for only humanity would rule the stars and soon humanity would annihilate the Keres once and for all.

And then their evil magic could be erased from the universe.

Maybe I should have given the Keres more credit though, I was basically naked at this point with only a thin purple sheet around me. I had no doubt it was covered in magic and the foul aliens were searching my mind, thankfully my training had covered those stupid basics so the Keres were never going to get my secrets.

The air was sweet and filled with hints of grapes, grapefruit and blood oranges. Yet knowing exactly how evil these aliens were they were probably the smells of their own kind that they were sacrificing to their own gods and goddesses, the Keres were beasts at heart.

At least the sweet smells left the great taste of fruit salad on my tongue exactly how my mother used to make it.

The sweet aromas got even stronger and I hated myself for daring to confirm the thoughts of the weird magic of the Keres. They were probably wanting to lure me into their mind games using smells but I was a human, I was righteous, I wouldn't be tempted by their witchery.

In fact I was just glad that I was okay and I sent off all my information to the wonderful Imperial authorities before these beasts captured me.

At least now the Imperium had a fighting chance against the awful predations of the Keres.

Let me tell you exactly what I sent them.

***

+++Transmission Recording+++

Dear Lord Eraser,

Apologies for the lateness of my call but these beasts are far more intelligent than we ever gave them credit for, they know what humans are and they actively hunt them down. We need to exterminate them as soon as possible, and how the hell we didn't annihilate them after the Great War is beyond me.

I am not questioning His wisdom just the consequences of the action.

I am currently laying on top of an immense purple crystal rooftop on top of the Keres version of a holy skyscraper. I have to admit I am more than impressed with the sheer straightness, perfection and smoothness of the sides of the building.

I had no idea creatures could make such a building out of pure purple crystal. This seems to be the location of where the Keres live, they create vast purple cities filled with these skyscrapers to live in.

At some point I might seek to gain entrance into these abominable buildings but I must be patient my Lord. I know the Keres might be tracking my transmission so by the Rex I must be careful.

For as far as I can see the buildings rise up like immense purple daggers veiling the sky, ground and mountains like each hab-block (though I doubt that is what these monsters call their buildings) are like fortifications. I will seek to access their weakness so if an attack is needed we can bomb them in their sleep.

Which thankfully my Lord I can confirm the Keres do need. It is currently midnight on the planet and there is much less traffic about. The bright purple metal pods that the Keres use as transports are far fewer right now than they were earlier. You should have seen them my Lord, it was disgusting, huge purple streaks of pods through the sky.

It was an abomination to humanity's birthright and was nothing compared to the holy whiteness of our shuttles. It makes me sick just mentally sending this to you.

The air stinks, my lord, of foul oranges, grapefruits and grapes. This I must investigate further to make sure this is a food source and not some kind of biological weaponry, but I will confess the sheer silence of the city concerns me greatly.

There are no sounds of their awful high-pitched language, no shuttles zooming about the rest. This is most unnatural and I will admit my fear of exploring this most alien of worlds is building.

I will continue my mission for the Rex.

+++Transmission Send+++

***

+++Transmission   Signal   Searching+++
+++Transmission Signal Found and Sending+++

Immense bangs, pops and explosions echo around me my Lord as I enter a huge purple crystal "factory". That is what this place must be because it is so different to all the other types of buildings I have explored so far.

This building like all the others is simply made from living purple crystal with little strange lights that pulse, swirl and twirl around inside. I feel like they are looking at me half the time and I hate these creatures, I hate aliens and I can feel the cold fearful sweat drop down my back.

I am a warrior my Lord. I am not a recon specialist but I do not seek to question the Rex.

The "factory" was amazing as I watched the long lines of purple crystals, metals and corpses float up in the cold air in long, long lines high above me. If any of those corpses were still alive then I would probably look like some random ant or something.

The factory was so huge and I was so tiny.

Yet it was the silence that still infuriated me. I was used to so much sound, so much noise, so much joy but I couldn't hear anything.

So I did the only logical thing my Lord and I followed the endlessly long lines for as long as I could. I followed it to a large purple crystal balcony that overlooked a stunning pit of some sort.

I was amazed at it because the Keres were here. So many evil, corrupt, demonic Keres were here and I had a weapon on me, but I had to focus on the mission.

Recon only.

All the evil Keres were so thin with their tiny waists, largeish chests and sharp pointy humanoid features that it was simply disgusting, and a perversion of the Rex's divine Will. It was disgraceful that these aliens ever believed the Rex would allow them to look so close to humans.

I studied the females in their long black dresses that swept across the floor with long blond pieces of hair floating up like the air and constantly moving, almost like they were scanning the air.

I just hoped these creatures weren't intelligent enough to detect me.

The Keres stood in their long lines and as soon as a shard of crystal, a chunk of metal and a chunk of a corpse floated past, they would simply click their fingers and in a bright flash of magical light they would become weapons.

I saw guns, rocket launchers and laser swords being created.

And by the Rex did this annoy me. These Keres actually dared to create arms, armour and evil weapons against the righteousness of humanity that was disgusting and I wanted nothing more than to simply slaughter them all.

This was in direct violation of the Treaty of Defeat that these pathetic creatures signed after they lost the war.

Then everything stopped.

All the Keres looked directly at me.

They thrusted out their hands.

Magical fireballs zoomed towards me.

I ran like hell.

The enemy knew I was here.

+++Transmission sent+++

***

+++Transmission Sending+++

Dear Lord Eraser,

I need an urgent evacuation and urgent military reinforcements sent to my location immediately. The problem is far, far worse than I ever could have imagined.

The Keres were more demonic than we ever thought possible.

After the Keres started to hunt me down, I managed to escape into some kind of sewage network and it was mightily impressive because all the waste created by this society is simply magically teleported down into the sewer tunnels and they end up into a conversion chamber.

Then magic turns the waste into something useful again.

Of course I had to kill three foul Keres males to get you that information but it was worth it, and the entire Keres race will hopefully burn for it.

Anyway my Lord, after I escaped I knew the Keres were going to use their abominable magic to hunt me down so I decided to invade their homes, learn some more information and hopefully learn a secret to their undoing.

Let me tell you my Lord, our reports and beliefs and information about the Keres living like plebs couldn't be further from the truth.

I'm currently leaning against a bright purple wall made of pure crystal in some of the apartments and every single apartment is open concept, open plan and open everything. I do not believe these creatures even know what a door is.

Instead of sofas, they had a strange orange floating thing in front of a row of pink diamonds, which I now believe is a type of communication network using their magic to power it all.

I tried to get the young Keres woman to show how it worked but she refused, so I killed her.

The kitchen area is even stranger my Lord, because there are no holo-freezers, holo-ovens or even a food synthesiser. There are just bowls of huge blue melons and I think the Keres just magic up their food and drink.

That is what another young man was doing before I stormed in and killed him.

It is no wonder these aliens are so dumb and inferior to humanity. Maybe these lazy aliens learnt how to cook instead of filling their bodies with magic then maybe their species wouldn't be as braindead as humanity.

Thankfully that just makes killing them easier.

But my biggest concern is the massive bright orange, glowing sack on the bright white ceiling. It concerns me because I believe there were small, baby Keres inside.

Every so often when the bright orange sack flashes, I can see small fingers, small legs and small faces just staring me at smiling, laughing and waiting for something bad to happen.

Of course I would never kill these baby Keres because that is not what the Rex wants. He requires baby Keres to be indoctrinated into the ways of humanity so they see their own species as corrupt and evil, and in the end the Keres will annihilate themselves and become slaves for humanity.

That is why the Rex is so clever because he is always so much further ahead of the enemy.

But this concerns me greatly because all these apartments that I have broken into have these orange sacks above them. I don't like this and this means that instead of the Keres population dying off like we believed.

It was actually growing and that means the Keres will soon be able to raise an army against us.

We must be ready.

Someone's coming.

+++Transmission sent+++

***

I have to admit I didn't expect the Keres to simply click their fingers and knock me out when one of their military commanders in their golden, ornate armour stormed and took me prisoner.

I just stared at the bright white lights flashing about in my purple prison cell as I realised that I shouldn't have been able to remember those things. I was an intelligence officer and my mind was a fortress and once I did something in the Rex's name I shouldn't have been able to remember it, much less recall it inside an enemy prison.

A sweet musical laughter echoed all around me as the purple drained away from the crystal to become see-through. I just frowned as I saw I was isolated in the middle of nowhere on some damn moon.

For as far as I could see there was only endless amounts of grey rock, there were no people, no signs of life and no other signs of prisoners. There was just me alone and I knew I was about to die.

I had read a lot of intelligence reports over the years and I knew how the immoral Keres worked. As soon as the crystal prison cell went away I would choke to death and I wouldn't be able to scream.

There would be no air at all.

The sweet aromas of blood oranges, grapefruit and grapes went away to be replaced with the cold smell of dust. Because in the end that was all what the galaxy was, one single massive sheet of dust, rock and death.

"Thank you for revealing your mind to me," a human woman said into my mind.

"I did not reveal anything to you, and why do you work for the Keres? If this is mental conditioning then fight back, fight for humanity, fight for the Rex," I said with authority.

The woman laughed inside my mind. "You are a fool little man because the Keres are innocent creatures that humanity were scared of. We slaughtered their race for nothing except fear and now I am making things right by helping them,"

"Traitor. Murderer. Evil woman,"

"Call me whatever you want but I know the truth Isaac and I know what is coming for humanity and the Keres. A force so great that only the Goddess Genitrix can save us,"

I just laughed at the stupidity of this woman, clearly she had fallen for the delusional ideology and mythology of the Keres. The idea that the Big Bang was caused by the birth of a Goddess of Life and a God of Death and the Keres were created to guard life and humanity was born to destroy all life and serve the God of Death.

It was stupid and I honestly pitted this pathetic woman.

"You can never change so I will release you from your fleshy body and I just pray to Genetrix that she grabs your soul before He does,"

I was about to protest out loud when I noticed the crystal prison cell was gone and I could no longer breathe.

"And thank you for the transmissions," the woman said. "They never reached the Imperium and I will always fight against your corrupt oppressive empire,"

My eyes just widened in horror as I collapsed gasping for air that wasn't there and I just hoped that the Keres would all die out because they were evil, I had seen that first-hand and I bore witness to their foulness because I had lived amongst the enemy.

And now I could happily die for my sins.

AUTHOR OF THE CITY OF ASSASSINS URBAN FANTASY SERIES

CONNOR WHITELEY

ALIEN'S MIND

A MATILDA PLUM CONTEMPORARY FANTASY SHORT STORY

ALIEN'S MIND

"Matilda, the aliens are back,"

When my best friends in the whole wide world, Jack and Aiden, said that single little sentence in perfect unison, I just looked at them because they had to be flat out wrong. Right?

As it was early April, the three of us were sitting in my massive therapy office with its wonderful bright white walls with stunning art on three sides and beautiful floor-to-ceiling windows overlooking Canterbury, England along the other side.

The three of us had all picked our seats from my rather large range of seating, that clients always thought was some kind of psychological trick but it was actually just to make them feel comfortable. I was sitting at my brown desk, Jack was sitting on a beanbag and Aiden was sitting on the floor resting his head on his boyfriend's lap. They really did make such a cute couple together and I really did love them too.

They looked even cuter with their matching jeans, white shirt and black shoes that I was fairly sure was more due to the fact their washing machine was broken than any planned matching.

Thankfully it was getting fixed today by a great friend of ours, but they still looked way better than me in my cream blouse, navy blue trousers and high heels I seriously couldn't walk in.

We were all meant to be going over the year's taxes and seeing how we could make sure we pay no tax whatsoever, because I always preferred to donate my tax bill to charities that actually did good work instead of the UK government.

As superhero psychologists, the three of us had all the superpowers of the myths and misconceptions about psychologists but because no one believed psychologists didn't have to pay tax. That was a superpower we were so missing unfortunately.

My office smelt amazing with hints of jasmine, lavender and oranges from a new smelly candle Jack had bought the practice because a superhero in the Candle Sector of the world was starting a new business. We were all too happy to help her out and it did smell amazing. It even left the warming taste of orange tarts on my tongue like my mother used to make in the 1900s.

Jack and Aiden were looking at me like I was meant to say something about their comment about aliens. I personally really wanted to ignore them because the last time I had dealt with aliens I ended up being a sex therapist to a small cube alien and I didn't want to go through that again. Not when I had taxes to do.

"They'll be here shortly," Jack said.

I just rolled my eyes because that was the problem with having best friends that always, always spent extra time with our boss Natalia learning the history of the Gods and superheroes and that just happened to involve aliens at some point. I knew I was going to have to learn it at some point but I was normally too busy helping people.

Then the alien appeared.

I didn't actually know if I was more shocked about the alien not being a small black cube, or if the fact it looked like an immense black snake troubled me more or less than the first.

I hated snakes with a passion because of my service during world war one and two but this alien was just scary. The alien had awfully long white fangs that dripped sweet-smelling venom onto my white carpet, its scales were a shiny black and the cold blood red eyes of the creature was very off-putting.

I wanted to shout for my boss to come and help me but considering I was the best superhero (her words, not mine) I was hoping I could handle this with my best friends.

The alien licked the air and just stared at the smelly candle like it was a demon about to kill it.

"Can you please remove *that* thing? It smells awful and soon my venom glands will start overproducing," the alien said.

Aiden looked at me and I nodded so he got up and blew out the candle.

"Natalia said you could help me," the alien said with one eye focused on me and another eye on Jack and Aiden. That was just creepy.

"How do you know Natalia?" I asked.

The alien licked its fangs before a large glob of venom could fall on the carpet. "Who do you think bought the Gods, Goddesses and Superheroes to this planet before you humans crawled out of the sea?"

That was amazing.

"We are the Creators, an alien race by your standards, that watch, help and aid all civilisations in the galaxy to thrive in this cold dark universe," the alien said. "We found the Gods on a faraway planet and that made us realise we needed to help them,"

"And Earth was the perfect home for them once humans crawled out of the oceans," I said wanting to sound like I was understanding this.

The alien nodded.

"So why are you here now?" Jack asked. "The Histories said that you tried to kill the Gods once they created superheroes and you've been banned from Earth and the Sol System ever since,"

I might have been a psychologist by trade but I could definitely fight if I needed to. I just didn't want to fight an alien.

"I've been experiencing some problems with a friend of mine and I reached out to Natalia and asked if she could help me. She refused because I tried to kill her once but she said it was her mission in life to help everyone. So she sent me to you,"

Now I really wished I knew what Natalia wanted me to do. Do I help him or turn him away?

As much as I wanted to turn him away because he was evil for trying to kill my boss, I just knew that I had to at least hear him out.

"What's the problem?" I asked not even trying to use my non-judgemental language.

He shook his head so I used my Trusting Superpower and he slowly nodded to himself.

"My girlfriend isn't herself of late and she wants to conquer our race and lead it for herself. She thinks everything everyone else says is stupid and she thinks she's a Goddess of some kind," the alien said.

I looked at Jack and Aiden because we had a massive problem. It was stupid of us to apply mental health conditions for humans to an alien race. Their psyches, mental processes and more were all different to ours so why did this alien think we could help him?

"Let me bring her to you in one hour and you can see for yourself," the alien said.

Before I could protest he disappeared and I just looked at Jack and Aiden. I had a very, very bad feeling about this and I only get these feelings before something truly horrific happened.

***

The next hour was incredibly tense in the office so much so that I had changed sitting at my brown oak desk for a blue sofa that I had tucked against a wall, and as much as I wanted to relight the smelly candle I couldn't because it would upset the damn aliens.

I liked aliens, I liked helping people but I always felt out of my depth in these sort of situations.

The only benefit of the past hour was that Jack and Aiden had told me everything they knew about this alien race and it was barely anything. Apparently, the Gods refused to record what happened and it had been so many millions of years that most people had forgotten about it all.

Even Natalia.

A few moments later the alien from earlier reappeared with his shiny black scales even shinier and this time he carried a much, much smaller black snake alien with bright sapphire eyes.

She looked beautiful in a weird alien sort of way but I could sense that something was wrong. I normally don't use my mind reading powers (that only work once a person has spoken to me) on aliens but I felt like I was going to need them.

The girlfriend laid on the ground perfectly still and grinned at me, Aiden and Jack before laughing.

"She does this a lot," the boyfriend said. "And my name's Bobley,"

"Matilda Plum," I said offering him my hand to shake before realising he didn't have hands.

"That's a stupid name Bob. You should have changed it like I said. You are stupid, weak, pathetic. I am the rightful ruler of the Creators and we need to create an army," the girlfriend said.

Bobley just looked at me. "She says this stuff every hour of every day like clockwork,"

I nodded and closed my eyes for dramatic effect as I started to read the girlfriend's mind. Like always I couldn't understand an alien's mind because it was way too different to a human mind, but I could *feel* her emotions.

Maybe that was enough.

I coursed through her mind using her feelings and emotions and rages to guide me. I saw weird images without sound, smell or any sensory details but that was to be expected in a way. The human mind did this a lot but my superpowers could easily bring it all together to give me a full picture.

Clearly my superpowers didn't know how to do that in an alien mind yet.

The images were of weird spaceships, maybe some planets and maybe some dreams but there was a repeating pattern emerging. This girlfriend hated her boyfriend for no reason.

Or no good reason that I can tell. She thought everything about him was pathetic, every idea he had was pathetic and she was planning to kill him as soon as today.

She had actually been "cooking" something to kill him but this little therapy trip had stopped her most evil plan.

I pulled out of her mind and she was just focusing on me.

"Your girlfriend hates you and if she was a human I think there's a good chance she's psychopathic and she could be narcissistic too,"

Jack and Aiden nodded so presumably they had been doing the same as me in her mind.

"Is there a cure?" Bobley asked.

I just shook my head and I hated it that everyone believed that mental conditions needed to be cured like they were diseased because they were diseases. But that was an argument for another day and one that I wasn't having with an alien.

"No, but we might be able to make some suggestions to her," I said, looking at Jack and Aiden.

They both stood up and sat next to me and we all interlocked our fingers to combine our power.

"I will rule our race. I will build my army. We shall conquer all the Created Planets for the Creative Empire," the girlfriend said. "And we will water the galaxy with the blood of our foes,"

Me, Jack and Aiden just closed our eyes and focused our powers into her mind. We could implant suggestions so deep to make her do exactly what we wanted her to and I just hoped her being an alien wouldn't stop this working.

It very well could.

I coursed through her mind and it was all blank now. I couldn't see any images, I couldn't smell anything, I couldn't feel any emotions. I could hear something though.

It sounded like thousands of human teenagers laughing, crackling and wanting something from me. The sound seemed to be everywhere and then it went silent.

I felt like I was being watched and I knew this was some kind of mental defence. We had to get out of here.

I didn't know how alien minds worked but I had no intention of finding out what defences they held and what happened to the people that got caught up in them.

"Implant suggestion now," I said.

I felt Jack and Aiden nod so we all combined our powers and suggested that whenever the woman wanted to conquer, kill or hurt anyone of her species or any living thing she could hit herself in the fangs. The most painful part of the alien's body.

We all withdrew just as I felt immense coldness start to crawl over us as some kind of mental defence was triggered.

When I opened my eyes Bobley was grinning and hugging and kissing his girlfriend again. He seriously loved her and that was great to see.

Then the woman flicked up her tail and lashed herself in the fangs again and again and again. Clearly all this alien thought about was pain, suffering and death.

Not exactly a lovable person so now maybe Bobley would see how truly monstrous the woman he loved was.

***

Three hours later after a massive amount of tax stuff, ordering coffee and pizzas on the business account to give to homeless people in secret and calling up every single Tax and Accounting Superhero I knew, we managed to finally get everything sorted so we wouldn't pay tax at all this year. And because we saved over a million pounds in tax, me and my two best friends could send hundreds of thousands of pounds each to our favourite charities.

I would probably send mine to an eating disorder charity this year because I had helped a ton of teenagers with eating disorders this past year so it was sadly a growing condition.

I blew out the smelly candle that I had been burning ever since the aliens left because I loved the smell so much and I did enjoy ordering more and supporting my fellow superheroes even more than I already was.

So Me, Jack and Aiden were all about to head out when a large holographic message appeared in front of our blue sofa that the two aliens had been in front of earlier.

I picked it up and I was shocked that it wasn't a message but it was a "newspaper" article about the execution of the female alien we had helped earlier. She had been executed for treason, intent to kill a Creator and terrorism charges.

Apparently after she kept lashing herself in the teeth, Creator Police had stormed her quarters to find the Creator equivalent of bombs, poisons and guns. She was planning a massive attack and the article credited three humans with saving the day.

I told Jack and Aiden and they just sort of smiled. I had to admit that this wasn't exactly great news but at least we had saved a group of aliens today that might have been killed in an attack.

Just as the three of us left the room I smiled to myself because my job was weird, wonderful and challenging, exactly how I loved it but even I had to admit that alien minds were the weirdest and certainly something I didn't want to explore again anytime soon.

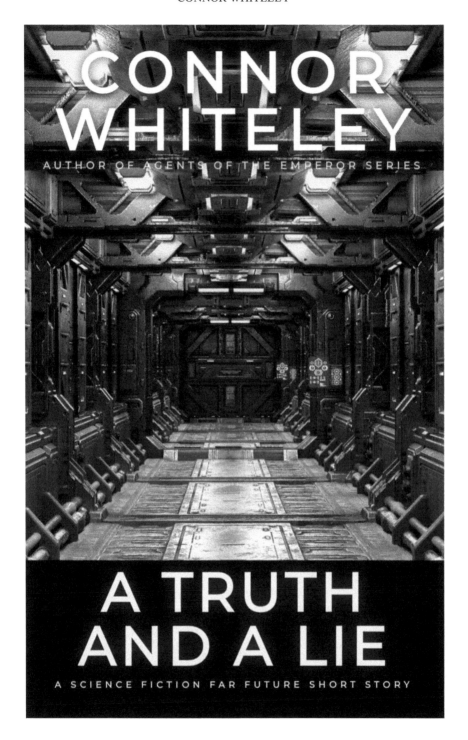

A TRUTH AND A LIE

If you asked any of the tens upon tens of trillions of humans in the Imperium how they would get access to forbidden knowledge, then there were only ever three answers. The most probable would be, they would simply report you to the authorities and you would never ever be seen again. The second answer would be you shouldn't because that is simply immoral and an affront to humanity and the Truth that the Rex lies about.

The third answer would be to find some kind of abomination like an alien, a historian or some kind of other forbidden creature that possessed such knowledge. The only problem with such things was that they were rarer than rare and you would most probably die in the process.

Thankfully that was not a problem for Commander Jerico Nelson.

Thick aromas of alcohol, sweat and wonderfully sweet chocolate filled Jerico's senses as he went inside The Lover's Bar onboard the disc-shaped space station known as Outpost-66.

Jerico smiled as he leant against the wonderfully warm grey metal doorway where a handful of people were coming and going. They were clearly military cadets judging by their cleanly pressed grey uniforms, and Jerico almost wanted to ask them where the hell they were off to.

It wasn't normal for any military units to be this far from civilisation, but he couldn't do that because he was hunted, keeping a low profile and he just couldn't draw attention to himself. And it wasn't like the military of the Imperium wasn't a massive Cult, if he spoke to the wrong person, then Earth would be told sooner or later.

Jerico shook his head at the very notion of Earth finding him.

Jerico hated how the entire bar was awful as a strategic position if anything went wrong.

The two rows of small metal tables pushed around the curved grey walls of the bar wouldn't provide any cover. But Jerico liked how people of all shapes, sizes and heights sat around the tables talking and laughing about their business. They were all drinking some kind of bright blue liquid that was probably strong enough to power small shuttles.

Jerico seriously didn't want to drink it if he could help it.

Jerico almost laughed as he saw three women in very attractive red dresses do some sort of exotic dancing on the oval platform in the middle of the bar. No one was paying attention to them so Jerico supposed their job was to simply get them in the bar.

But Jerico really didn't need them to get him in the bar.

Jerico went towards the massive bright red floating counter towards the very back of the bar. He clocked everyone was slowly looking at him, trying their best not to be seen, but he had been a Commander in the Imperial Army, he knew the signs of being watched. Jerico just needed to know how to find some forbidden information on a target and then he would leave all of these people in peace.

Most of them would hopefully be too drunk later on to remember him.

The closer he got to the counter the louder the humming, banging and popping of the space station got, it had faded as background noise so it was only now Jerico was realising the noise was still there. He still didn't like it, because it could easily hide the footsteps of enemies.

He gave the very tall woman behind the bar a friendly smile, but he was laughing more at himself than her. He just couldn't believe how obsessed he was with strategy and knowing how to win in a fight, he knew the skills were useful but they always popped up at weird times.

The woman smiled at Jerico as he leant against the icy coldness of the counter. The smells of oranges, lemons and grapefruits filled his senses making the great taste of lemon tarts form on his tongue.

"You want something that isn't alcohol, don't ya sweetheart?" the woman asked in a way that surprised Jerico. She sounded like she knew a lot more than Jerico wanted her to.

Jerico looked around the bar. All he wanted was a little information on where some human woman called Ithane Veilwalker could be, he had no idea what she really was. He was only going off what he had been told.

Jerico didn't believe for a single moment she was some woman who had been killed and brought back from the dead by some alien Goddess, but he had been gifted a task by a dying friend and he wanted to see it through.

"You seek someone," the woman said.

Jerico laughed and shook his head. He had no clue how to ask his question to this woman but he doubted she was as innocent or human as she appeared.

"I know if you want forbidden information then it is always best to start in the most remote regions of the Imperium," Jerico said keeping his voice as low as possible.

The woman smiled and nodded and Jerico looked around again and noticed a tall man wearing a black military uniform near the front door was watching them.

"Clearly I am not the only person who knows that little fact," Jerico said.

"Of course not," the woman said dropping her human-accent for just a moment.

Jerico took a step back and really looked at the woman. She looked so human with her thin waist, fat cheeks and long brown hair that she should be human.

But after a few moments, Jerico realised she was an alien Keres. He noticed how her ears might not have been pointed but they had been cut to remove the points, her waist was unnaturally thin and her facial features were all too perfect, too pointy, too human to be believable.

Jerico instantly wanted to reach for his pistol on his waist to protect her. Everyone in the Imperium knew to kill a Keres on site if they were found but Jerico couldn't allow that.

He had murdered way too many Keres over the decades out of blind obedience for him to let another human make the same mistakes he had.

Jerico leant very close to the Keres woman. "They will kill you if they find you,"

"I know," the woman said. "That is why the Man In Black is here. He had heard of magical miracles happening in this sector, I heal people you see who shouldn't be healed, so he came to investigate,"

"And now he wants to kill you," Jerico said hating the entire damn situation with the Imperium.

"If you help me escape then I promise you I will help you with whatever you need. Yet I need to know the topic,"

"I need to know where is Ithane Veilwalker?" Jerico asked, nodding.

The woman reached down below her counter and started to look like she was mixing drinks of some sort. Jerico really liked the intense aromas of orange and lemon and grapefruit but she was clearly acting.

The Man In Black was watching them intensely.

"Ithane Veilwalker is a myth created by your Imperium to give us false hope. The Keres are dying and we are being slaughtered by your Imperium. We want peace and you people enslave us,"

Jerico shook his head as he felt his necklace (that was apparently meant to contain the Soulstone of the Keres Goddess of Hope, Spero) pulse warmly around his neck.

Jerico took out the necklace and showed its bright blue jewel to the woman. "If that is a myth then why is Spero wanting me to find her?"

The woman's mouth dropped and Jerico could see she was conflicted and awed and even in a little fear as a drop of sweat rolled down her hand.

Then the woman laughed manically.

Jerico took a few steps back and whipped out his pistol.

The woman's veins turned black, black oil poured from her mouth and Jerico cursed under his breath. She was a Keres alright but she was a Dark Keres. She had sold her soul to the Keres God of Death Geneitor, a divine being devoted to the destruction of all life.

Or so the bullshit stories said.

Jerico aimed. He fired.

Bullets screamed through the air.

The woman laughed as she ate them and her arms transformed into immense black talons dripping dark red rich blood.

A scream came from behind.

Jerico spun around. He saw men and women run out of the bar screaming and shouting warnings as they went.

Space Station security would be there quickly. Jerico had to find his information soon.

The Black In Man charged at Jerico.

The woman flew forward.

Jerico rolled forward.

He fired at the Man.

The bullets bounced off him.

Jerico leapt up. The woman swung her talons at him.

Jerico blocked them. He punched her in the face.

Icy coldness shot up his arms.

The Man fired at the woman.

She screamed.

She shot out her arms. Black fire engulfed him.

He screamed in agony.

Jerico fired at the woman.

Tendrils of black fire melted the bullets but then the Man's screams just stopped and everything went silent.

When the silent flames finished crackling and engulfing the man, Jerico gasped as the Man was just a skeleton made from black crystal.

"Kill him," the woman said.

Jerico fired.

A bullet screamed towards the skeleton. It smashed into him. Shattering the crystal.

Jerico scanned the bar for the woman. She was gone.

He carefully searched behind the counter. He could sense her foul dark magic here. She was alive.

He just couldn't see her.

Jerico felt his heart pound in his chest. He felt sweat drip down his back. He could feel his fear responses kicking in.

Then Jerico's chest filled with the warmth of hope that Spero provided him with. He calmed down and he closed his eyes.

He wanted to sense the woman.

Air rushed behind him.

Jerico jumped forward. He opened his eyes.

He just missed two immense talons.

He fired into the air but he didn't hit anything.

Jerico closed his eyes again. He couldn't rely on human senses to find a Dark Keres. He had to rely on instinct.

Air zoomed towards him.

Jerico leapt to one side.

He felt the intense rush of heat flow past him. He wanted to panic at the idea of almost being cooked alive so he didn't allow himself to.

The air churned around him.

Jerico ducked. Fired three rounds all around him. He kicked the air.

He heard a scream as a bullet smashed into something and then his feet kicked the Keres's head.

Something cracked and Jerico opened his eyes to see the damn Keres woman collapse to the ground gripping her stomach as black blood poured out of the wound.

Jerico pointed his pistol firmly at her head but he was surprised that she was truly smiling at him. Her veins had returned to normal and Jerico had no idea how these Gods worked but he almost believed she had been freed of Geneitor's corrupting influence.

If such things actually happened.

"You helped me escape Geneitor. Thank you," the woman said weakly.

"Where is Ithane Veilwalker?" Jerico asked.

"The Father of Death knows. He tracks her but he only allows me to tell a lie and a truth before he claims my soul,"

"Speak and die then," Jerico said hating that he was being mean to a Keres that had probably only fallen to such corruption to survive humanity's onslaught.

"Ithane seeks the history of the Soulstones or Ithane can be found in the grave on Earth," the woman said before she died.

Jerico shook his head. It was clear that Ithane was alive, his old friend wouldn't have sent him on this mission if she could be found in a Grave so it was good to know he was looking for some History thing.

But Jerico just grinned to himself. His next task of following Ithane in her search for History was going to be next to impossible, everyone in the Imperium knew the Real History of everything was impossible to find.

The Rex had rewritten history thousands of thousands of times depending on what he wanted his human subjects to believe, so finding the True History of the Soulstones and anything related to the Keres was going to be next to impossible.

But as Jerico left the bar and looked for a shuttle to steal (ideally one that couldn't be traced), he was really excited for the future because this was going to be a hell of a mission and he truly loved impossible missions.

Especially when they involved hunting down impossible information and sorting fact from fiction in the crazy universe that was the Imperium.

AUTHOR OF AGENTS OF THE EMPEROR SERIES

CONNOR WHITELEY

ASHES OF VALICAN

A SCIENCE FICTION FAR FUTURE SHORT STORY

ASHES OF VALICAN

An entire world was burnt to ash in a matter of minutes.

When I, Elizabeth Sobeth, was summoned to investigate the events of Valican, I hardly doubted it was anything more than a simple case of a planet being miscategorised by the idiots of the Imperium and their so-called divine Rex.

What I actually found terrified me.

According to scans, maps and a number of highly rated travel books, I should have been standing in the middle of a luscious ocean with amazing colourful fish, monsters and tourists would come here for months at a time to sail on these stunning seas.

Believe me that couldn't be further from the truth because I was standing in the middle of an ash-covered stretch of land that really did go on endlessly for miles upon miles. There was nothing here for ash that was constantly getting blown up and kicked into the air by a harsh warm breeze.

The ash was an interesting mixture of black, grey and yellow that constantly swirled around each other in weird alien ways that I didn't understand.

I wanted to believe it was nothing more than damage from a massive fire but considering that there were no signs of life, no signs of water and no signs of anything on the planet, I knew I was just hoping for the impossible. Something or a group of people had killed an entire planet.

Thankfully, after I made my full report to Earth and the Rex himself, this would all be out of my hands. Because the very last thing that I wanted to do was deal with a group of aliens or humans that had the power to burn an entire world.

The sheer smell of ash, smoke and charred flesh filled my senses and clawed at my lungs. I wished I had bought my damn rebreather but that was impossible because I had left it on my black ship in orbit.

Something that I really didn't like about the planet besides the smell and walking on ash, was the sheer silence of the planet.

I had read the reports and documents in Imperial Records and this entire planet had hosted over two billion humans, it was a fairly advanced colony and the people were making a killing off the tourism trade.

So who could have done the annihilation of an entire planet so easily? There wasn't a call for help, any survivors or any sign that anyone knew what was happening.

I went off into the distance, hating how soft and crumbly the ash-covered ground felt under my feet and my stomach twisted in a painful knot at the idea of the ash collapsing and me falling into a pit.

That was a very real fear.

The sky was remarkably clear considering the sheer amount of ash on the ground. The sun was shining brightly off the intensely light ash so I was more than happy I was wearing a holo-visor, protecting my eyes from the intense UV light, and my robes were long so I shouldn't burn.

Yet I feared that burning and going blind were the least of my problems.

I kept walking through the ash covered wastelands, just hoping that I would find something to tell me what had happened.

I always carried a small black box device that allowed me to take air and ash samples but I had done that earlier. The air was perfectly okay and the oxygen levels seemed to be increasing oddly enough despite the lack of trees on Valican.

"Do you know me?" a voice said behind me.

I stopped instantly because no one was there a minute ago so I turned around and jumped.

A woman was sitting there.

I just focused on the tall, very thin woman just sitting there like she was dying or something. I knew she was from the planet because she was wearing the traditional long white robes of this culture and golden rings were wrapped around her neck. One for each of the so-called Great Beasts she had killed.

Apparently on Valican there were ten Beasts that a person needed to kill to be ruler of the planet. The Rex had always found that detail funny so he allowed the humans to continue that weird tradition even under his tyrannical rule.

And yes I do realise everything I have already said in this report is more than enough to get me executed for treason against the Rex. But oh well.

The woman had nine of the rings around her neck and her face was smiling but her lips were cracked and her eyes were glassy. She was blind and she was looking right at me.

And I could have sworn she was staring into my soul.

"I don't know you," I said. "I am Doctor Elizabeth of the Imperial Science Division,"

"Are you here about the monsters and the Space Children?" the woman asked.

I hated how I had to remember every single little detail about this weird culture. She knew that the Rex normally burnt worlds for believing in any being besides him but this world had humoured him for some reason.

I wish my own home planet was that lucky.

"What are the Star Children?" I asked.

"The creatures you call the Keres that came down from the skies in screaming pods of purple, black and blue. They howled and roared and screamed bloody murder in the name of their dark God Geneitor," the woman said.

Valican grabbed her stomach. She felt it knot and churn

violently. She had faced the Dark Keres before, magical alien beings that wanted to resurrect their God of Death so he could wipe out humanity and save the Keres race from annihilation.

Annihilation that humanity had unjustly started. Again that simple sentence would so get me murdered by the Rex.

"What happened here?" I asked kneeling down on the ash-covered ground so I was at least eye-level with the woman. She followed my gaze perfectly.

It was so creepy.

"We were all just minding our own business. I was feeding young girls in the market and listening to them talking about dates they were going on later tonight. That is when the sun went out for a minute as the pods of the Dark Keres screamed out,"

I jerked backwards slightly because this woman wasn't what she was pretending to be, because not a single human outside of the highest levels of Imperial government and rarely the Imperial Army knew there was a difference between the Dark Keres, Keres and the Daughters of Generatrix. Another offshoot of the Keres race that wanted to resurrect their Goddess of Life to safeguard the Keres race.

"Who are you?" I asked.

The woman grinned. "A trickster some say. A monster others say. What do you call me Doctor Sobeth?"

She knew who I was. That couldn't be possible and that was just wrong on so many levels.

"You want to tell me what you and your people did to this world," I said knowing this foul alien probably wanted to kill me as much as I wanted to kill it.

"We needed souls for Geneitor. He was hungry and our warband was interested in burning a world for the fun of it and we wanted to unleash the Incarnation,"

I shivered at the very mention of the Incarnation. I had heard it mentioned a lot of times in hushed voices when I was serving alongside a detachment of Imperial special forces.

No one had ever seen the creatures but the rumours were powerful enough. It was said that once there were enough murders, spilled blood and screams on a battlefield that The Champion of Death could summon a shard of Geneitor's soul into the galaxy.

In the form of a demonic monster known as the Incarnation. A creature so powerful, monstrous and deadly that entire armies could explode in minutes.

"Did you summon him?" I asked really knowing I had to find a way to kill this woman before she killed me.

"No," the woman said sounding disappointed. "That was not what caused the death of your world. The death of your world was more sudden than a simple battle and I know the Dark Keres were not behind it,"

I shook my head. She had to be lying. The Dark Keres had attacked this innocent human world so the killers had to be them. Right?

"You are a clever soul Doctor. You know I can sense Geneitor wanted to lick and taste your soul so you will be killed at some point. I know that would make my Master happy but you must look closer to home to find out who had murdered your people,"

She charged.

Jumping on me.

She punched me.

Fangs shot out of her.

I gripped her fangs.

They glowed blood red.

Burning my hands.

I snapped them.

Thrusting them into the woman's head.

The woman laughed loudly as I killed her and I kept stabbing her until she didn't laugh anymore.

But if what she said was true then I needed to return to my ship and research if the Imperium had ordered this murder.

And if the Dark Keres had simply come here to feast on the

souls because they knew the humans were already going to die.

***

As much as I didn't like my small, cramped research ship that was nothing more than a black circular sphere with only one room in the entire ship, I had to admit that it did have excellent research capabilities.

I sat in a giant black metal chair holding a small holo-reader as I scanned Imperial archives of what had happened to Valican over its lifetime and what top-secret projects were rumoured to live here.

The rest of the ship was only the size of a swimming pool but it was filled with so many holo-readers, pieces of research equipment and food containers because I wasn't allowed a food synthesiser there was barely any room left for me.

I hated the ship almost as much as I hated the Rex himself.

Anyway, the archives showed that Valican was once a death world because it was so far away from the sun that it couldn't possibly support any forms of life. Yet these are exactly the sort of worlds that the Dark Keres love to hide on.

When Valican was first encountered by Imperial forces, they found two warbands of Dark Keres on the surface, so they were murdered and the planet suddenly became filled with trees, animals and oceans.

At the time no one cared because this was right after the Treaty of Defeat was signed so the Keres race had lost the war, humanity was basically subtly enslaving them and the human race was safe whilst they continued to murder a peaceful species.

But I now believe this was a trick done by the being known as Geneitor to lure humans to the world so he could kill them at a later date.

I had to sadly readjust myself in my metal chair because the icy coldness of space was seeping more and more into my ship. That meant the damn heater and engine systems were failing.

I didn't have long left to discover the truth before I had to flee and stop my search.

However, as much as I like that theory I have to admit it is wrong. Since the problem with Imperial Records on Geneitor is even though I have heard rumours of the Rex acknowledging the existence of the Keres God and Goddess he refuses to allow research on them so the majority of humanity did not fall to their corrupting influence.

I sort of understand that.

Anyway, the small amount of data I can find about Geneitor is that he never ever creates life. He only kills it so the idea he could create an entire planet filled with trees just to lure in humans seemed impossible.

So I believe humanity used a terraforming technology that was not documented and that led to the creation of Valican.

A much more likely theory has to come from the Lord Planetary Governor of Valican himself because before he was assassinated and the Rex himself directly ruled over the planet, he confessed to a series of nuclear experiments.

Since the Planetary Governor wanted to learn why and how humanity had almost annihilated Earth before using this technology. And as much as the Rex's supporters claimed the ruler of humanity cleared out the planet of nuclear waste, I know the Rex would never do that.

A weapon is a weapon and nuclear weapons would be like the best present ever to the Rex.

There's no way in hell he destroyed them so there is a good chance these nuclear weapons went off during the attack of the Dark Keres.

I readjusted myself in my chair yet again as I shivered and I noticed my breath started to form long columns of vapour. I was running out of time before I had to make a jump to somewhere safe.

I flicked over the page on my holo-reader and I realised what had actually happened to this planet and I realised just how evil the Imperium was.

Back in the Keres-Human War, I had helped and studied and built the supernova Destroyer Class warships that had a weapon so powerful that a single blast could destroy an entire planet in a second.

Of course that warship was thankfully annihilated by the Keres towards the end of the war but the technology always remained. In fact, I had seen the technology used in everything from guns to missiles to laser weapons.

And an old boyfriend had told me that the supernova technology had recently been changed to superheat a planet and the Imperium was looking for testing sites.

Of course he wanted to know what planets I wanted dead, I said none, so I later found out that the Imperium had killed my ex-boyfriend for failing to find a planet. The Imperium was extremely weird like that.

A superheated blast would be more than possible to burn an entire world and if the Keres legends about Geneitor and Generatrix being able to sense life and death were true, then I have little doubt the God would have sent a warband there to make sure they collected the souls on his behalf.

I shivered at the very notion of what I had discovered and a small red flashing light appeared on my holo-console. I knew it was an Imperial Navy warship coming to kill me because that's the thing about the stupid Imperium.

You cannot say something against them. you cannot challenge them. And by the Rex, you certainly cannot discover the sheer power they hold because that means you know something they don't want you to know.

Meaning they cannot control you enough.

So I spun around on my black metal chair and with shaking hands I simply typed in coordinates to the Enlightened Republic, the little breakaway region of humanity that believed in peace, democracy and working with the Keres against the predations of the Imperium.

When I entered the Ultraspace network, a warning light told me three missiles were heading my way.

I zoomed off into the network and I was really looking forward to starting a brand-new life in the Republic, learning more about the

Dark Keres and helping to protect humanity from both itself and the dark powers that stirred in the divine.

Lines were being drawn and sooner or later a massive fight between humanity, the different divisions of the Keres and the Republic would happen. And I just hoped for the sake of the innocent, that the right side won.

The ashes of Valican would always remind me why fighting against the Imperium and the Dark Keres were the most important things imaginable.

CONNOR WHITELEY

DEATH OF A FAMILIAR

A SCIENCE FICTION FAR FUTURE SHORT STORY

DEATH OF A FAMILIAR

Today taught me why humans couldn't be trusted because this was the day I died for my Goddess.

The last thing I would ever call humans is normal. They are strange, complex and very smelly creatures with their soft flesh, large waists and they are just weird to look at.

I had met many humans over my long life on many worlds that I mostly forget now, but the story of humanity and their species is all the same. War, killing and blind ignorance of the truth about the universe.

And I should know to be honest because as I curl up in my wonderfully soft purple Familiar bed, that a bastard human had once decided to call a "cat bed" as if I was such a low life as a cat. I was a Familiar of the Keres race, a cat-like creature with much more beautiful, softer and striking purple fur given life by the Goddess Genetrix herself. I was not a cat.

But yet I digress, my apologies.

You see I was all nice and toasty and curled up on my bed, allowing the wonderful warmth that my magic pulsed into the velvet fabric, to travel back into me. It was like sitting on a warm metal chair without the intensity of the heat. I loved it.

I rested my little head on the edge of the bed and stared out at my boss's new room that was oddly human and I hated it. considering my boss was a Keres, a much thinner, pure and magical version of humanity created by the Goddess of Life Genetrix millions of years ago, I didn't understand the human decorations.

The office itself was a massive grey metal box in my opinion with weird orbs of bright white golden light floating near the dark grey ceiling. The little orbs were pretty to look at as they bounced along the ceiling causing shadows to dance across the grey floor.

The entire office just looked cold and isolated and not Keres at all. I had always loved the wonderfully dark purple, red and blue crystals that the Keres manipulated to create whatever their impressive minds could develop. By contrast human design just always felt a little lacking.

My boss was sitting at her ugly massive desk that was an immense slab of grey metal with some cute Keres items on them. I noticed she had a glass bowl of blue glowing crystals that she had placed a magical shield over to stop me devouring all those delicious treats at once.

She was crafty like that.

But I could sense my boss was tense, nervous and her single claw tapped loudly against the metal desk.

She had developed that clawed finger way before I was gifted to her by the Goddess but it had apparently happened during a spell gone wrong. She had wanted to cast a torrent of fire at some humans that were going to kill some innocent people but the spell backfired.

She tried to focus too much magic through a single finger so the finger exploded, killed the humans and saved the innocent but the finger had twisted into a claw.

A cold, dead, awful-looking claw.

"Do you sense the humans yet?" my boss asked me.

I wasn't even sure why my boss wanted to see a whole bunch of smelly humans today in this awful office. Even the hints of human coffee, caramel and toffee that stunk out the air was out of place and I might have been lending my magic to create the smell but it was still out of place.

The only benefit was the great taste of toffee that formed on my tongue. I did enjoy it when humans brought me treats like that.

"Tazzie," my boss said, "do you sense the humans?"

I closed my eyes briefly and coursed my magic through the immense crystal-like ship we were currently on. The banging, humming and popping of the ship tried to interfere with my senses but it failed.

I felt the darkness of the Death God Geneitor press against my mind but I couldn't allow the Great Enemy to stop me. I coursed my magic through the entire ship and then I detected the dull glow of human souls boarding.

"Of course," I said almost offended my boss actually believed I wouldn't be able to. "I still do not understand the importance of seeing the humans in *this* place,"

My boss stood up and I admired her long blond golden hair that framed her sharp, pointed face and ears perfectly.

"These humans are not from the Imperium and they do not serve the Rex. They could be allies in the fight to save the Keres,"

I didn't bother moving my head because I was comfortable and enjoying the warmth far too much to risk moving. But I still rolled my eyes.

I really did like my boss and I was grateful for the Goddess to gift me to her, but she was an idiot at times. The tyrannical awful Imperium and that monstrous Rex, their leader, would hunt down every single element of the Keres they couldn't manipulate or control. And then one day they would want to wipe us all out.

It was simply the truth.

The Death God wanted to obliterate Genetrix's creations and he was using humanity to do it. Yet because humanity refused to believe in the simple truth that the two divine beings existed, they were walking themselves further and further into damnation with each passing day.

I doubt these humans would be any different.

"You doubt me?" my boss said.

I grinned and tried to hide my fang-like teeth from her. "Of course I doubt you. I doubt your entire race at times because of what you allowed to happen and continues to happen,"

My boss stood up perfectly straight as we both realised the humans were coming closer to the office.

"The main Keres race might be happy living by the monstrous terms of the Treaty of Defeat that means we're slaves to humanity but I will not allow that. It is why I serve the Goddess as a Daughter of Genetrix,"

I nodded and smiled as the cold metal door of the office hissed open and three humans walked in.

I covered my nose with a purple paw as the foul aroma of sweat, blood and human waste filled the air. I am sure they wouldn't have smelt to other humans but I was a Familiar and my senses were extreme.

Even my boss didn't seem to notice too much.

Boss clicked her fingers and three very human wooden chairs appeared. I was disgusted in how simple and artless the humans were about their chairs. It was a crime against the beauty that Genetrix placed in the world but I had to behave.

"Who is the cat?" one of the humans asked but at this point they all looked as weird as each other.

"Tazzie is not a cat. She is a Familiar gifted to me by Genetrix, Creator of Life,"

I rolled my eyes and leapt from my bed to the desk making all the humans jump.

I stood there as Boss continued to introduce the mission of the Daughter of Genetrix and how they wanted to protect both the Keres and humanity from the predations of Geneitor.

I rolled my eyes again at the humans but they were all wearing bright baby blue military uniforms and I could sense there was darkness in each of them. It wasn't a massive amount of darkness or even something to be alarmed about, but something wasn't right.

"Why is the Familiar looking at us?" the human to my left asked.

"Her job is threefold. She is meant to protect me, amplify my power and serve Genetrix however she sees fit," Boss said.

I stared at the human. "And sometimes that means killing whoever attacks us,"

The humans smiled like I was some type of domestic play animal that couldn't possibly hurt them.

"We have been sent here by the Enlightened Republic to support you in exchange for you helping us," the tallest human said taking out a something large wrapped in black cloth.

I hissed as soon as I sensed the darkness and Death Magic pouring out of the black cloth.

I flashed my fangs at the humans but again they didn't seem concerned at all. They were more focused on Boss as she hissed and wiped her nose like trying to wipe away a bad smell.

The human placed the object on the desk so I backed away and smiled as even the desk groaned in protest of having something so dark on it.

"So the humans bring us a Death Object," I said through clenched teeth. That had to be a foul crime itself and it was outrageous that the humans had discovered such an object in the first place.

No wonder I had sensed Darkness in them. The mere exposure to such an object would cause Geneitor's influence to take root in their mind, body and soul.

"This is outrageous, Boss," I said. "The Goddess would never allow this object on one of her ships,"

Without warning the humans took off the black cloth and they made sure a small piece of the cloth touched my paw.

The cloth burned my paw and turned the purple fur to ash. I shot backwards hissing in agony.

The air crackled with purple magical energy around me but Boss raised a warning finger at the humans and I knew she would deal with the situation.

Yet I understood why she hadn't killed the humans for now because if there was a Death Object in play then we had to deal with it and find out if the humans were a real threat or not.

I slowly went over to the bowl-like object that had been covered by the cloth and I flat out hated the weird shrieking sound that echoed inside my head. I knew the damn humans wouldn't have been able to hear it, but then again me and Boss were sensitive to this stuff.

In fact every single Keres on the ship was probably hearing this and having the Darkness try to influence and push into their minds, bodies and souls.

I didn't want to have this aboard any longer than needed but there was something weird about the design.

This particular Death Object was a large black bowl made from a strange type of glassy stone with millions of lines of writing. It was clearly Keres writing from the shape but the little black tendrils coming off the bowl made it hard to read.

I wasn't sure if those tendrils were natural or if the Goddess was trying to protect us from the evil writing.

"What is a Death Object?" a human asked.

"The stupidity of humans never ceases to amaze me. It is amazing you primitives can even begin to understand the grandeur of the universe," I said flicking my two tails harshly.

"Come, come now Tazzie. The humans are silly in their beliefs for sure but there is power in their ignorance. They are likely to be corrupted by the Death magic which this bowl serves as a container,"

"The question is what do the humans want us to help them with?" I asked staring at the tallest of the humans.

The humans grinned. "We need you to help us destroy it because it is making a madness spread over an entire world in the Republic,"

I gave Boss a sideways glance. It wasn't unheard of to hear about such an event happening, and I know there had been plenty of victims of Death Magic over the past tens of thousands of years.

But no humans or even Keres could touch a Death Object without falling under its corrupting power.

Boss held her hand over the surface of the bowl and bright white magic crackled in the air and I lent her some of my strength.

I could sense her magic trying to tap into the Darkness to study it, see what could happen and to see if there was a spirit we could fight.

But this was a unique Death Object that made the foul aroma of charred flesh, hair and death fill my senses.

"How did the humans touch this without fall to the Darkness?" I asked knowing it was impossible.

The humans looked nervously at each other. "We made a deal with a man that appeared when we touched the bowl,"

I prepared to pounce and Boss magicked a long purple sword out of thin air.

The humans grinned and they spoke as one. "It was a good deal for humanity. They sold their souls to me and in exchange I allow them to take the bowl off-world,"

Boss shook her head and I sensed her psychically battling with the Death creature that had clearly possessed the poor stupid humans.

The humans took a few steps back and I watched the humans and Boss stare into each other's eyes. There was clearly going to be as much a war of words here as much a psychic battle I was going to help with at some point.

"Why allow them to take the Bowl off-world?" Boss asked focusing on the humans intensely. "It makes no sense because you could corrupt millions of souls so why settle for three?"

"Because the humans would come here," I said staring at the bowl as the dark tendrils started to shrink back. Probably because the Death Creature had to use their magic in the mental battle with Boss instead of using it to protect the bowl.

That meant it was weaker.

Boss screamed out in pain and gripped her head as the Creature striked a mental blow.

I lent Boss all the strength I could.

Boss thrusted out her hand. Flattening a human against a wall. Bones cracked and organs exploded painting the walls of the office in dark red blood.

The other two humans laughed as their skin turned deathly black and their veins glowed sickly yellow.

The humans charged into each other and became one twisted, deformed walking corpse that made the air crackle with black magical energy.

"Death Creatures I hate them," I said my tails flickering around wildly.

I hissed as loud as I could sending the magical soundwaves slamming into the Creature.

Boss flew at the Creature. I had to do my part. I couldn't fight it. I still had to help Boss.

I spun around and focused on the evil Bowl. It was glowing dark evil black and I could sense the Darkness start to take root in the hull of the ship.

That had been the bastard's plan the entire time. Keres souls were brighter, purer and so-called tastier than human souls. So Geneitor planned to corrupt the ship inside out so he could force an entire ship's worth of Daughter of Genetrix to fall to his worship.

It was monstrous, pure monstrous.

I raised a paw. My claws shot out. I striked the Bowl.

Crippling pain filled me. My bones moved violently and I felt like my paw would shatter.

The Bowl hissed in pain as I realised how weak and helpless the Bowl was. It wasn't made from stone it was made from the dreams and delusions of the Death Creature.

It wasn't real. It was an abomination on the Goddess's work.

I clawed it again.

A massive chunk of it turned to ash but I was in agony. I was in so much crippling pain that I couldn't hiss or meow or do anything.

I tried to raise my claws again but I couldn't. I was in too much pain.

Boss screamed.

I spun around. Sending two fireballs at the Death Creature

allowing Boss to jump up and slash at his chest a little.

Pure magical energy filled me from the Goddess because I had to do this, I had to annihilate the bowl despite the pain but I couldn't.

But I had to do my duty.

I striked the bowl but my paw collapsed into the bowl like it had been eaten and all the pain receptors had been consumed.

I just looked down at my poor little paw as it was no longer there and I felt the corrupting influence of the Darkness pulse up my arm and my heartbeat flooded my body with the corrupted blood.

I felt the warmth and wonderful life that the Goddess filled me with start to become more distant as her power was fading from me.

Boss screamed as she realised I was dying and the Death Creature laughed.

I screamed in defiance and charged at the Bowl. The dark tendrils shot back in fear and I smashed into it with such force it flew off the desk.

Smashing onto the ground below. Turning to ash.

The Creature hissed and screamed out in a deafening roar as it started to dissolve because it couldn't remain in reality without an anchor. Something I had just annihilated.

As the threat was dead, the humans were no more and the ship was saved from Geneitor's corruption, I collapsed to the ground as my paws and body were slowly devoured by the corrupting Darkness that had taken root within me.

"At least Genetrix will grab my soul before Geneitor can torture it forever," I said trying to smile but accidentally flashing my fangs.

I could see how badly Boss wanted to touch me, cuddle me and stroke my blackening fur a final time. I would have loved that too but she couldn't become corrupted herself because the ship needed her, the Daughters of Genetrix needed her and most importantly the Goddess needed every able servant ready for the war to come.

Geneitor was growing stronger and stronger and if he reached full strength then he would happily devour all life in the galaxy and then the universe.

Something none of us could allow.

"I love you," I said to Boss. "You're a good woman, a good fighter and hell of a Servant of the Goddess,"

She smiled and I noticed a small crystal tear start to form in her eyes and she went to say something else.

But as the Darkness continued to dissolve my body and ears, I never heard the words but I knew they were words of thanks, appreciation and love. Because I might have been difficult at times but we were Familiar and Boss, a match made in the heavens and a bond that couldn't be broken because it was stronger than love and I really did love Boss.

And I was more than happy to have died to save her, the Keres and all the innocent people they would go on to save in the name of Genetrix, Goddess, Creator and Protector of life.

CONNOR WHITELEY

DIVINE KNOWLEDGE

A SCIENCE FICTION FAR FUTURE SHORT STORY

DIVINE KNOWLEDGE

"Impossible. The knowledge you seek is divine, forbidden and dangerous,"

Of all the sentences, Commander Jerico Nelson had suspected to hear as he sat down on a beautifully large golden throne-like chair, it certainly hadn't been that. He had wanted to come to the forbidden Enlightened Republic for the first time ever and he had wanted their help.

They were supposed to be the champions of Freedom, Democracy and everything the tyrannical Imperium wasn't, and yet they were still wanting to hide knowledge from him. Knowledge that might have been able to save everyone they loved and all of humanity.

Unless the Imperium finally launched an invasion of the Enlightened Republic and all of humanity killed each other in the process. Jerico seriously hoped that never ever happened, but it was only a matter of time.

Jerico just shook his head and he forced himself to look away from the ancient-looking elderly lady sitting at her oak desk in front of him. He liked how her long grey hair still looked full of life, joy and she was clearly healthy but she was just annoying him.

The entire chamber was actually rather good and Jerico really liked the beautiful yellow stone the high walls were made of. He wasn't too familiar with this particular type of stone but its shininess, strength and size certainly would have made it excellent cover to hide beneath in case of an attack.

Even the holo-art hanging on the yellow walls were impressive and Jerico was just happy he was here. The elderly woman might have been annoying, but this was the Enlightened Republic. It wasn't perfect but at least he could and probably would say whatever he wanted without getting arrested for simply disagreeing with the leadership.

"I will not give you any knowledge without permission," the elderly woman said as she stood up.

Jerico enjoyed the sweet aroma of roses, oranges and cloves that filled the air as she moved around, searching the immensely tall bookcase behind her.

Jerico watched her closely in case she was going to reach for a secret weapon or something. He seriously doubted she would but he couldn't be sure these days. He was already a former military Commander being hunted down in the Imperium for apparently betraying humanity.

He seriously couldn't believe the bullshit the Rex had spread about him. He wasn't a terrorist, a monster or a danger to the very fabric of the Imperium. Jerico had only realised decades too late that the alien Keres they were murdering were actually great, innocent people.

Humanity was only killing the Keres because humanity was scared of their innocent magic. Jerico hated the Rex and all the idiots that kept him in power.

"No," the woman said to herself as she searched through some of her books.

Jerico looked around and he was only going to give her a few more minutes before he forced the matter. He was searching for anything he could get his hands on about the so-called divine objects known as Soulstones.

He didn't believe in the Keres Gods or Goddesses at all (which even he admitted was odd considering he had been gifted a Keres necklace that was meant to the Soulstone of the Keres Goddess of

Hope, Spero) and apparently the Soulstones contained the souls of the Gods and Goddesses of the Keres.

But he didn't buy it.

And as much as he wanted to just forget about these damn Soulstones, Jerico wasn't going to fail his old (dead) friend for a single moment. His friend had sent him on a mission to find some human woman that had been reborn by the Keres Goddess Genetrix and he was going to find her.

That search all rested on him finding out about the history of the Soulstones.

"I need that knowledge," Jerico said standing up, surprised as the taste of orange chicken formed on his tongue. It was one of the most amazing things Jerico had ever tasted.

"Do you like the taste?" the woman asked.

"What is this trick?" Jerico asked looking round for any food he might have missed. There wasn't any.

The woman laughed. "I am Knowledge Chief of the Republic. There isn't a single piece of history that flows through the Republic that gets past me,"

Jerico really enjoyed how the sensational taste of fruitiness orange and fresh chicken got more and more intense.

"So what is this orange chicken thing? Is this some kind of knowledge?" Jerico asked, not sure he wanted to know.

"Of course. There was a tribe about three thousand years ago that developed technology to manipulate the taste of their enemy's mouth to disarm them. It was very useful before the tribe killed them,"

"I am not your enemy,"

"I do not know that. In fact there has been a full squadron of Death Troopers watching and following you ever since you alerted us to your presence,"

Jerico paced around. "Surely that proves I am no threat to the Republic. And the Republic has spies in most corners of the Imperium, you must know they are hunting me as much as they can,"

"It could all be a deception and come on Commander, when has a Commander of the Imperium turn their back on the Rex?" the Knowledge Chief asked deadly serious.

Jerico laughed, not because it was funny, but because she was absolutely correct. Jerico had no idea if anyone in the history of humanity had ever betrayed the Rex. He personally handpicked each and every one of his Commanders and they had to be extremely brutal, murderous and some insane things to grab his attention.

Jerico hated himself for what he had done. He had burnt entire planets of Keres warriors before, or were they all warriors? Jerico knew those planets contained families, young people and so many innocents but he never questioned his orders.

Because what does the lives of some alien scum matter?

Jerico just looked at the Knowledge Chief. "How do I redeem myself? And how do I prove I am no threat to the Republic?"

The woman only grinned and Jerico couldn't help but get excited because this was going to be a very tough mission indeed.

***

Jerico flat out couldn't believe the sheer darkness of the long tunnel the Knowledge Chief was leading him down. He wasn't a massive fan of the immense yellow sandy blocks that made up the rough walls with bright almost blood-red cement filling the gap between each block.

Jerico wrapped his fingers round his pistol just in case this was some kind of trap, but as much as he didn't want to admit it, he just knew the Knowledge Chief wasn't going to kill him or trap him or do anything untoward.

He got the sense that she needed him for something, a task that no one had been willing or stupid enough to do.

Jerico kept following the Knowledge Chief down the tunnel, listening to his own awful breathing that he was trying and utterly failing to keep under control. The more he tried to focus and control his breathing the worse it got, and Jerico just focused on the Knowledge Chief.

He was almost surprised she was so confident, elegant and powerful considering how old she looked. Jerico didn't think she was wearing any technology or had any work done to her, but this was the Enlightened Republic. He wasn't too sure of the level of technology here, so anything was possible.

The wonderfully strange aroma of coffee, chocolate and strawberries filled Jerico's senses, making the delightful taste of strawberry shortcake form on his tongue, but then the Knowledge Chief stopped.

Jerico looked past her as a stupidly warm breeze brushed his cheeks and Jerico just knew that something wasn't natural about the tunnel.

Jerico looked at the Knowledge Chief who was grinning at him, almost like this was the last time she was ever going to see him. He was going to see her again no matter the cost and Jerico was going to survive this.

He hoped.

"What is this task then?" Jerico asked, not liking how the woman hadn't spoken to him for ages.

"This tunnel was originally created by the Keres when this world was owned by them. Then Geneitor unleashed a death curse on the world and there is a creature here that stirs," the Knowledge Chief said.

Jerico took out his pistol and shook his head.

"You might wonder why we haven't found the creature but the answer is simple. We have sent twenty men and women down here and none of them have returned. But I want to know what the Creature is and how to stop it from killing anyone else,"

Jerico nodded as he checked the sight on his pistol. "Actually my question was why build an entire human colony on a Keres Death World?"

The Knowledge Chief laughed. "Because only three people in the entire Republic know this is a Death World. Not even Supreme General Abbie knows this world's origin,"

Jerico wanted to argue with the Chief, because surely it was critical for the President of the Republic to know everything about her domain. But Jerico supposed that wasn't his problem, if the Republic relied on the same pack of lies, deception and falsehoods to remain as bound together as the Imperium. Then he didn't want to be here any longer than needed.

"I'll find the Creature for you but I am not killing it unless I have to," Jerico said not really knowing why he felt that way.

The Chief sighed and simply walked away.

Jerico went further down the hallway and enjoyed the wonderful warmth that flowed around him. He felt Spero's necklace pulse extra warmth into him and he knew this was a deception.

His footsteps echoed loudly in the hallway, a lot louder than they had a moment ago, and he could feel Spero trying to help him.

He still didn't believe in the stupid Keres Gods and Goddesses but whatever the magical thing in the necklace was, it wasn't trying to kill him. Which he seriously appreciated.

After walking down the hallway for a few minutes and the wonderfully intense aroma of chocolate, coffee and strawberry got even stronger, Jerico stopped as he felt like he was being watched.

He closed his eyes for a moment and then he opened them to see a man standing in front of him.

It was clearly a Keres man. His long pointy humanoid face was ghostly white, his ears were like daggers and his massive grin made Jerico uncomfortable. It was even worse that the man was unnaturally thin even by Keres standards and Jerico couldn't see any weapons.

That concerned Jerico a lot more than he ever wanted to admit.

Jerico blinked and he found himself standing in a hallway that was three times wider. It wasn't natural but nothing about Keres magic was. He couldn't allow himself to die.

"I am not an enemy," Jerico said with as much authority as he could.

The Keres man nodded and he started circling Jerico so Jerico did the same. When the Keres man took a step closer, Jerico took a step back and vice versa.

"I am aware of who and what and where you are, but who am not aware of why you are?" the Keres man asked.

Jerico shook his head. He hated some Keres, they were just flat out weird at times.

"I'm here to find out information about Ithane Veilwalker. Do you know her?" Jerico asked taking a few steps forward so the Keres took three steps back

"Of course. The Reborn, the Daughter of Genetrix, the Unpure Keres. Of course I know of her the entire galaxy sensed her Rebirth and everyone searches for her,"

Jerico wasn't sure he liked the idea of that. If this Ithane woman really was as important to the survival of all life in the galaxy, then Jerico hated to imagine what the Imperium would do to her if they found her. Let alone what the Dark Keres would do, the servants of the very Death God she was meant to obliterate.

The Keres man took four steps forward so Jerico did the same backwards.

"What do you know about her?" Jerico asked.

The warm air crackled with black magical energy. Jerico aimed his pistol at the Keres' head.

"Humans, always so focused on weapons and murder and death when I have the information you need. When Geneitor burnt this world and left me alive to warn others of similar sins he gifted me knowledge and power and magic,"

Jerico aimed his pistol right at the man's forehead. "I have seen the gifts that Geneitor spreads and it all ends with corruption and death. Tell me what you know and I might let you live,"

The Keres man laughed. "Live? Life? I am a servant of the God of Death. I do not care about life but now the Father of Death hunts you too. You have appeared in too many places not to be a threat,"

The Keres man screamed.

Jerico fired.

The Keres charged.

Bullets bounced off the Keres.

The Keres's arms became swords.

He swung at Jerico.

Jerico rolled backwards.

Jerico leapt up.

Firing his pistol until it was empty.

The Keres laughed.

The bullets screamed through the air.

Smashing into the Keres.

The bullets smashed onto the ground. They did nothing.

Jerico rolled his eyes. He hated this. He hated Dark Keres. Bullets were always useless.

The Keres leapt into the air.

Spinning around.

The air crackled with magical energy.

An invisible force gripped Jerico.

He tried to move. He couldn't.

His necklace glowed bright gold.

The Keres screamed in agony.

The force released him.

Jerico charged at the Keres.

Smashing his fists into the Keres.

The Keres hissed.

Jerico gripped the Keres's wrists.

Snapping it over his knee.

The Keres screamed in crippling pain.

Jerico whacked the Keres in the mouth.

The alien fell to the ground.

Jerico grabbed the alien by the neck and raised him over his head and smashed the Keres man over his knee. Shattering the Keres's spine.

An icy cold blast of air whipped past Jerico before he saw himself back in the same width of the hallway he had been in when the Knowledge Chief had left him, but the corpse of the Keres man was gone.

"He wouldn't have killed too many more people you know," a man said behind him.

Jerico looked behind him and frowned as he saw a floating skull. "What the hell are you?"

The skull laughed. "I must keep this short because I cannot control things in your reality for too long. But that Creature only would have kept killing humans whenever a human was stupid enough to enter the tunnels,"

"But the Chief Knowledge mentioned in passing these tunnels were sealed," Jerico said.

"Young adults, young couples and even the adventurous old always find a way into restricted tunnels so he killed them and fed me the souls," the skull said rotating to the left.

Jerico took a few steps back as he realised he was speaking to some sort of strange version of Geneitor, or at least that was what this skull wanted him to believe.

"You aren't Geneitor so go," Jerico said aiming his empty pistol at the skull and just hoping the skull didn't realise how empty the threat was.

The skull laughed. "And so my wife places the fate of the galaxy in a human woman and a man that doesn't believe in the Divine battle he is walking into. Oh this will be fun my love. Let the Games begin,"

Jerico was about to punch the skull when it fell to the ground and turned to dust.

Jerico couldn't help but feel like he was entering a war on a scale he couldn't even begin to imagine.

And he wasn't sure if that scared or excited him a lot more than he ever wanted to admit.

***

A few hours later, Jerico leant on the massive oak desk in the Chief Knowledge's office as she just sat there looking, smiling and humming at him. She still looked as ancient as she did earlier but Jerico had to admit she looked good knowing he was alive and successful on his mission.

Her hair was still full of life, joy and looked healthy so clearly life in the Republic wasn't so bad even if the city and colony were built on a Keres Death World. Something Jerico fully intended to share with someone at some point.

"Do you have my information?" Jerico asked. "I need access to the Soulstones records,"

The Knowledge Chief laughed. "We don't have any records pertaining to such forbidden knowledge,"

Jerico slammed his fists on the desk. He hated this stalling, he hated the Republic, he hated how everyone was trying to stop him on his mission.

"Because the records never existed in the first place at least not in a manner that humans could understand," the Chief Knowledge said.

Jerico looked around the entire damn office in frustration, hoping that there was a book or something he could grab or steal just so he could find some answers. But the entire silly chamber was just as good as it looked earlier with its beautiful yellow stone walls and impressive holo-art.

She really was telling the truth.

Jerico wanted to argue but he knew, just knew she was telling the truth. There probably were records available in the galaxy about the Soulstones but they were probably written in Keres or ancient Keres.

Something none of them could understand and even though the Republic protected the Keres as much as they could, Jerico doubted the Keres would be too willing to share such knowledge with them. Especially with the constant threat of Imperial spies.

"But," the Knowledge Chief said, "if I have learnt one thing in my long life about the Keres, it is that their magic runs on emotion and it is that emotion that will lead you to your goal,"

Jerico went to laugh but he hissed in pleasure as Spero pulsed loving warmth into his heart. And Jerico realised that he had a good idea where to find the Soulstones or at least find Ithane Veilwalker.

If he was a Keres God or Goddess (creatures that didn't really exist) then Jerico supposed he would feel safe on the world famous for where they apparently walked.

"Genesis," Jerico said. "The so-called Mother World of the Keres, the world where the Gods and Goddesses first walked on Holy ground,"

Jerico was rather impressed that he actually knew that, but he was fairly sure Spero had implanted some of the information in his head.

"And it is said that where their bare feet touched the ground ten thousand gemstones reaching to the planet's very core was planted," the Chief Knowledge said grinning like a schoolgirl.

"Bullshit, surely?" Jerico asked.

The Chief Knowledge laughed. "The Mother of Life has destined you for greatness but it will be a journey that will test you for sure. Now go dear Traveler because you will not be the only person to make this connection, darker forces now turn their gaze to the Mother World,"

"And soon another battle will be fought," Jerico said knowing exactly the sort of rubbish so-called mythic people tried to place.

Jerico nodded his thanks to the woman and as he went out of the chamber he felt pure excitement fill him because he was almost at the end of his journey. Once he found Ithane Veilwalker and made sure she was okay, he would have done his dead friend proud and he could go back to his old life of being hired protection and he wouldn't have to deal with anything more about the Keres, their Gods and their magic.

But he couldn't deny the chance of that was slim to none and that made him more excited than any guy had any right to feel.

AUTHOR OF AGENTS OF THE EMPEROR SERIES

CONNOR WHITELEY

DAGGERS OF FAITH

A SCIENCE FICTION FAR FUTURE SHORT STORY

DAGGERS OF FAITH

"We're approaching Sandor now, my Lady,"

I, Lady Ithane Veilwalker, smiled as my first-mate's wonderfully smooth, slightly high-pitched voice echoed all around me. His voice echoed perfectly off the brightly glowing purple walls of my chamber and I couldn't help but feel more and more excited about our destination.

"Thank you," I said into the air knowing full well that my blade-like warship's communication system would pick it up and send it to the bridge. "Send all the available data we have to my chambers and I want regular updates,"

I liked the warmth of my chamber as the purple crystals glowed brighter and brighter as the magic within them got excited about our destination. The air was wonderfully sweet with hints of honey, toffee and caramel like I used to have as a child back on Earth. I had loved those days with my family.

The lights in the purple crystals twirled, swirled and whirled around each other. and I had to admit, I flat out loved being reborn by Genetrix, the Keres Goddess of Life and Creation. I was starting to understand why she had resurrected me and wanted me to be her will incarnate. I loved life, I wanted to protect it and wanted to make sure that life endured no matter what.

It was why we were here after all.

A lot of my fellow Daughters of Genetrix, both human and Keres, couldn't understand why I had chosen a room so deep and dark inside the *Lady Of Light* as my chambers. I was her Chosen I could have made any chamber my domain.

But I might have been her Chosen, a demi-goddess some might even say but I never want the power of Genetrix to corrupt me and my purpose. So I allow my friends to have the nice places and this chamber isn't really so bad.

When I first came here the small box-room had smooth dirty grey walls and stunk of petrol, sweat and cheap sex. It was a small room that was screaming out to be loved, so that was exactly what I did.

Now smooth purple crystals line the walls and every single surface that it touched. I am surrounded by the quiet voices of the Keres and the other aliens and creatures that have pledged themselves to Genetrix. I can hear voices and Keres on planets on the other side of the galaxy, and I absorb all this information.

I'll never lie or ever dare tell anyone this, but it is a lot. It is so much information, so many voices muttering around me and I know I am barely able to maintain my sanity because of the amazing gifts that Genetrix had given me during my resurrection.

I focus on some voices for a moment talking about the Soulstones and I smile because that is exactly what all of us are searching for. It is why we were here and that is why I want to get down to the surface as soon as possible.

The loud hum, bang and pop of the engines filled my chamber as the entire fleet started to slow towards Sandor's orbit. I guessed we would be within launch range in a few minutes and the entire fleet would want to know my orders.

Sandor isn't the type of planet anyone normally visits. To say it's on the very edge of the Milky Way galaxy is an understatement, I wasn't really sure it had ever been touched by intelligent life until I felt the warm, loving touch of Genetrix correct me.

It turned out the sandy yellow isolated world had once been home to a small race of Keres. They were isolated, abandoned and they didn't want to worship Genetrix or the God of Death Geneitor.

They wanted to be free, but that didn't happen.

The Keres on the planet were wiped out for some reason and no life ever returned to the world. And that is what I don't understand, the entire fleet and my entire network across of million worlds were all searching for signs of Soulstones, the shards of the fallen Keres Gods and Goddesses dedicated to life and the death ones. These shards were so damn powerful that they cause the very planet they're on to morph and warp in magical ways.

But Genetrix had led me to this planet and I have no idea why.

An entire bunch of purple crystals melted away for a brief instant as a very tall human woman walked in wearing some thick metal armour that I hadn't seen in decades. She must have looted it from a corpse somewhere, but her raven black hair certainly made her look good.

"My Lady we have completed our scans and there are no life signs. No signs of Keres's culture and no signs of Dark Keres too," she said, her voice wonderfully soft and careful like she was hiding something.

I could feel myself wanting to use my magic on her to find out what was wrong but I didn't. Everyone was loyal to me and I was happy that there were no Dark Keres about. I didn't need those foul Keres that worshipped Geneitor here.

"What else?" I asked stretching and I couldn't believe how great it felt to release the pressure in my aching muscles.

"There is a structure down on the planet. It's small, not very important but your name is spelt out on it. The structure is at least twenty million years old but *Ithane Veilwalker* is the name written on it," she said.

I grinned. At least that answered the question about why Genetrix had wanted me to come here, she wanted to find out why the Keres culture on the planet had written my name an extremely long time ago.

"No life signs?" I asked not understanding what had happened to the original Keres culture.

"Negative, but I suggest we get moving my lady. Our officers tell me there is an intense solar storm preparing to be released in three standard-hours,"

I nodded. That wasn't ideal because it didn't give me much time to explore but then again, that was the great thing about modern technology. I could leave it until the three-hour mark and simply escape the system into the Nexus and avoid the solar storm.

"Orders?" the woman asked.

I nodded. "I'll go alone but maintain contact with me at all times. And... something feels off, watch the other planets in the system and make sure there are no Dark Keres in the system,"

I could tell the woman wasn't sure why I was being so careful but no one just wrote a name down twenty million years ago on a dead world at the very edge of the Milky Way galaxy for no reason.

Something massive was going on here and I just had no idea what it was.

No idea at all.

***

After portalling on the planet, the first thing that struck me was the sheer silence of the entire world. It could have been because I had spent so long, so many days and so many weeks in my chamber listening to the mutterings of people on a million worlds. But actually I think it was because of something else.

After my bright purple portal closed behind me, I stood on dark yellow sandstone in the middle of nowhere. Behind me in the far, far distance there were some sort of mountains that looked like tiny yellow toothpicks set against the sheer flatness of the sandstone ground.

Behind me looked like a massive drop as if I was on top of a cliff-like structure, but it was what was in front of me that really captured my imagination.

It was simply a large orange stone circle. Ten immense chunks of orange stone were neatly arranged in a circle so perfectly that I doubted anything other than the Keres could have done it, so at least there was some limited evidence that the Keres were once here. I still didn't understand what had happened to them though.

An icy cold breeze brushed my cheeks and originally I had assumed it had come from the planet but as three other breezes covered me I realised it was coming from the stone circle.

Each breeze had a slightly different aroma but the scent of blood, death and decay was certainly growing more and more intense. None of this was making any sense because the Keres on this planet had forsaken Genetrix and Geneitor. I just don't understand why there would be any divine influence on this world.

I went towards the stone circle and I placed my hand on an icy cold stone chunk. I closed my eyes and tapped into my powers hoping they would illumine the situation for me.

Nothing happened.

Not a single image, phase or voice echoed into my mind. I didn't feel cold so I knew Genetrix was still with me but it made no sense why her insight wasn't being shared with me.

I suppose it was possible that even the Goddess of Life and Creation had her limits, but I doubted it.

I walked around the immense stone chunks and stopped at a small opening between them and I noticed there was an altar-like thing in the very middle. It wasn't made of bone, wood or stone. It was actually made of daggers covered in black oil.

There were letters on top written in the blood of a Keres that spelt my name, and it would have been the magic in the blood that we had detected in our scans. But I cannot understand why these Keres knew my name twenty million years ago.

I went inside the circle.

And the most intense wave of coldness washed over me as the golden light of Sandor's sun turned black, screaming filled my ears and a million voices laughed at me.

I clicked my fingers and my sword didn't appear in my hand. I was alone without any magic, weapons or divine protection here.

"She's here," a million voices said.

"She's going to die," another million said.

"She's going to become a Dagger," one single male voice said.

"What are you?" I asked channelling as much authority and power into the question.

The blood written letters glowed bright red and I went over to them. They rearranged themselves rapidly and I felt someone appear behind me.

I moved to one side so I could still see the constantly moving letters out of the corner of my eye. But I could still see the person or creature that appeared.

I recognised the twisted, demonic form of a Dark Keres instantly. The Keres were always beautiful, extremely thin and tall and just unnaturally humanoid in all the ways that humans could and would never be. They had extreme agility, they were nimble and their charm was unmatched, but when a Keres fell to the God of Death all that beauty was twisted for Geneitor's own amusement.

This one was different though.

He didn't seem as corrupted and injured and mutilated as the other ones I had sadly met. This Keres was injured but his form seemed to be constantly shifting like he couldn't keep himself together.

"Who the hell are you?" I asked.

The Keres laughed. "I am ancient but young. Beautiful but ugly. I am your hope and your death,"

"Speak plainly or by Genetrix I will slaughter you without a second thought," I said.

The creature laughed. "How? You have no power Ithane. You have no magic, no help, no way to communicate with your fleet. They are getting very worried about you, they are scared, they cannot contact you,"

I shook my head as I realised this creature wanted my forces to come down here and look for me. The Creature wanted my forces here and I could figure out why.

"I don't know what you are but you created this entire situation to get me here. And I bet I can guess why. You knew I could bring you the chance of escape off this world," I said knowing that all evil aliens love that idea.

"Of course," the creature said. "When I learnt about the Keres I learnt about your story. I spoke with Geneitor and Genetrix through their stupid prays and I learnt the truth,"

I screamed as I watched the creature transform into a perfect copy of me holding an oily dagger.

He pointed the dagger at me. "I learnt that you were the one that could give me the entire universe. Genetrix cannot hear you now. She will never know that I killed you and I became you. She will give me unlimited power and then I will kill her and Geneitor both,"

Fear gripped me. I had no idea who he was but for some reason and I hate myself for admitting it. I knew he was telling the truth. He really could do all of these things.

"And then I will conquer humanity, the Keres and then I will conquer all the galaxies," the creature said. "Oh those stupid Keres if only they hadn't prayed in their darkest moment. I never would have found them from my cave,"

An intense wave of icy coldness came over me and the awful aroma of death, blood and decay filled my senses. I forced myself to focus on the creature but my eyes watered and my vision blurred.

I saw him charge at me.

I leapt to one side.

He grabbed my hair.

Ramming the blade into my chest.

I screamed out in utter agony as the blade slashed my heart.

I gasped as he released me and I felt against the dagger altar with the letters constantly swirling about.

"I serve the Goddess," I said. "She protects life as I do, she protects the living as I do. I am her will incarnate and I will protect all life,"

The creature laughed behind me. "Say as many religious doctrines as you want Human-Keres woman. You will bleed out and you will die either way. The old Keres fell to my influence after praying to Geneitor so your own faith will be your death,"

I could feel my magic and life force drain away from me but I still forced out a smile and I noticed the letters started to slow down and form words.

"What's so funny?" the creature asked.

"I don't pray. I don't pray and neither do any of my forces and you forget something about Genetrix and Geneitor. They may hate each other. One may be the Goddess of Life and the other may be a God of Death but they will never allow themselves to be tricked by an idiot. They want to kill each other and they will never allow anyone else to interfere with the Great Game,"

The creature shrugged and I simply pointed to the brand-new words that had appeared on the Altar.

"Have Faith," I said as I read the words aloud and I ripped out two blades from the altar. "I believe in Genetrix and I will never stop serving my Goddess,"

I stood up perfectly straight as I felt the warmth, love and magical power of Genetrix feel my senses and body again. My stab wound and heart healed itself and I just looked at the stupid creature that had tried to copy me.

"You might be some ancient evil lurking on this planet trying to find a way off this world but I am not your ticket and I know you cannot survive in space,"

The creature's eyes widened and let me tell you it is creepy seeing your own eyes widen in utter fear.

I charged at the creature.

The creature tried to react.

It was too slow.

I rammed my dagger into its chest.

I rammed the other dagger into its stomach and I twisted the blades as the creature dissolved.

Then the bright golden sunlight of Sandor returned and I just smiled as I saw hundreds upon hundreds of small purple ships zoom towards me. My forces were coming and I was finally going home.

***

A few hours later after searching the entire fleet to make sure the evil creature was well and truly dead and talking to Genetrix to make sure I had actually defeated the creature once and for all (thankfully I had), I sat on the wonderfully warm floor of my chambers, cross-legged.

My chambers smelt amazing with hints of oranges, cloves and lemons and I was joined by three humans in white robes and three Keres in blue robes. Apparently there was some sporting competition going on later that human vs Keres and then later on there were going to be mixed competitions, which I always preferred, but right now I was in "Pray" with my friends. Everyone who swears themselves to Genetrix is my friend or to be honest, family member and I love them all.

But I couldn't help but feel like my ears were burning for some reason.

"We still can't find any Soulstones," a human male said in a strangely thick accent.

"True," a Keres woman said. "We have to find the Soulstones if we ever hope to resurrect Genetrix to her full power,"

As everyone broke off into talking about their own theories, hopes and dreams about finding different Soulstones, I couldn't help but smile as I realised this was what I loved about my fleet. They were so wonderful, so dedicated and so committed to bringing about the resurrection of Genetrix so she could finally murder Gencitor once and for all that I couldn't help but feel proud to be their leader.

"I've found a Soulstone," a woman's voice said.

I waved my hand to silence everyone and I focused back on the purple crystals that were glowing intensely now. I clicked my fingers to amplify the voice so everyone could hear it.

"Report," I said.

"I am Leanne Oaks in the Enlightened Republic and there is a human man wearing a Soulstone around his neck. He says he is hunting you and he believes you will be on the world of Genesis. He has a Soulstone. We have to find him,"

"What is his name?" I asked.

"I do not know but he seems very interested in hunting you down. I cannot confirm if he is friend or foe,"

"Thank you. Continue your mission and may Genetrix guide you to your destiny,"

"And may she guide and protect you to yours," Leanne said before I closed off the connection.

"Orders?" everyone said.

I just grinned and I felt pure excitement fill my body because this was the moment I had been waiting for for ages. I finally had a lead on the location of a Soulstone and that meant I was one step closer to bringing my Goddess back to her full power.

"Tell the fleet to head to Genesis immediately. Summon all forces. We head there now," I said.

But I couldn't deny that the world of Genesis was a strange choice. I doubted the human man would have chosen that world because no one besides the Keres really knew about it, so why did the Gods and fate and destiny want me and him to meet on that world of all worlds.

I didn't know the answer but I was seriously looking forward to finding out. Whatever happened next I didn't doubt that it was going to be explosive, deadly and a lot of fun.

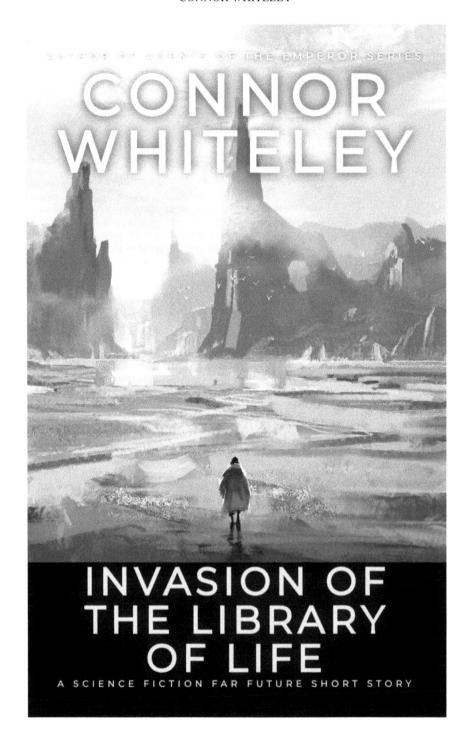

AUTHOR OF AGENTS OF THE EMPEROR SERIES

CONNOR WHITELEY

INVASION OF
THE LIBRARY
OF LIFE

A SCIENCE FICTION FAR FUTURE SHORT STORY

INVASION OF THE LIBRARY OF LIFE

The thick aroma of smoke, charred flesh and death clung to the air as I leant against the icy cold white marble railing of the balcony I was using as my position. I, Ithane Veilwalker, enjoyed the small amounts of coldness flowing up my arms and into my soul.

The entire balcony itself was rather good for watching the surrounding forests considering it was a wide semi-circular marble platform used for academics, readers and other scholars. In normal times they would have read out here and studied their texts and ancient books in the bright sunlight.

That wasn't happening anymore.

I was completely alone on the balcony today and there weren't even any small crystal tables or chairs that had covered the balcony when I had first arrived a few days ago. There were still the little cuts, slices and chips in the floor where people had removed the tables and chairs, but they were so minor it hardly mattered.

The entire tower, or Library of Life as it was called by the locals, was a place I had always wanted to visit. The entire tower was created and handcrafted from a solid immense block of beautiful white marble with stunning gold veining coursing through it like a river.

I was even more impressed with the thousands of ancient leather-bound books that lined the white shiny shelves inside. I had never seen a real book before, most of them had been burnt and annihilated when the evil Rex had risen to power and conquered the Imperium.

Books really were special things to all of us remaining humans because we knew the key to our freedom and saving humanity was written in our past. The past that was burning down around us.

I smiled to myself as the taste of barbeques formed my tongue, my parents had always liked them with my siblings and our large family. They might have been all dead now but they had given me an amazing childhood.

A massive roar ripped through the air and I just shook my head as a bright red missile flashed through the sky smashing into the immense forest in the distance.

The sky was veiled in smoke, ash and little white pods called shuttles. I knew exactly why the Imperium was invading this world and killing my friends. They wanted to kill me and see what I knew about the Mother of Life.

I never realised that being resurrected by an alien goddess and being made into her Will incarnate would make me so popular with the monsters of the galaxy. But Genetrix wanted me on this world and thankfully I had a friend translating an ancient text for me now.

I felt Genetrix pull on my mind a little and I knew that I was running out of time. The Imperium would breach the world's defenders soon enough and then they would kill me and the knowledge of the text would be lost forever.

Of course I could easily open a portal and just leave but the text was too fragile to move and my damn translator wouldn't leave this planet. Some rubbish about their soul being bound to the world, I hated how magic worked at times.

"My Lady," someone said behind me.

I rolled my eyes as a Keres man came up to me. His alien humanoid features were perfectly thin, a little gaul and elongated. His body looked way too thin for a human but that was so common amongst the Keres.

Genetrix might have created the Keres to protect life and her evil husband might have created humanity to kill all life but they were basically the same in the looks department.

"Yes Tau'Koo," I said feeling Genetrix really trying to pull on my mind. There was something the Goddess wanted me to realise but I just couldn't understand at the moment.

"The orbital defences are wiped out and the ground defenders are weaker now. The Imperium has landed in the North and South of the planet and Keres lives are being slaughtered,"

"Damn it," I said. I might have been 100% human with the powers of a Keres but I had never wanted the Keres to die. They were good, amazing people that had to be protected, but my presence had brought the enemy to them.

I needed a new plan.

"How much longer does the Translator need?" I asked.

"Another twenty minutes at least but which-"

I waved him silent because I knew exactly what was going to happen in the next twenty minutes, this world was going to die.

"Then let us see what power the Mother can gift me," I said closing my eyes and connecting to Genetrix and letting her presence feel my mind.

I tapped into her power and started to course over the immense forest below me with my mind's eye like how a bird might fly towards a seed on the ground. I needed to find the leader of the invasion and I needed to buy us time.

I found him.

I connected with his mind instantly. He wasn't a good man by any stretch of the imagination but he was skilled in hunting, killing and torturing Keres. I didn't need alien magic to realise that because I could sense the crystallised magic of his former kills.

Even now I was surprised that if the Keres were tortured for long enough their bodies would discharge their magic and connection to their patron God in an effort to save their life. It never worked but it didn't stop the biological processes of the Keres from doing it.

"I see you monster," I said echoing the words into his mind and hoping I could force a reaction of some kind.

I felt his thoughts turn happy that he actually wanted this and he had been expecting this.

"Where are you abomination?" he asked, "and tell me, what thoughts can you see?"

I didn't like it how he knew about the mind-reading ability Genetrix had gifted me. There had to be a spy amongst my gang and that was a major problem.

I didn't stop though, I could see his past and abuse from the family that was meant to love him. I could see how the Keres had robbed him of the chance to ever see if his parents could love him (they never were going to but he didn't realise that) and I could see his name.

He was Bloodheart.

The name almost forced me to kill the connection. Everyone in the galaxy knew who Bloodheart was, I wasn't even sure he was real or just a myth to keep the Imperium scared. He was a murderer, a butcherer and capable of burning an entire planet for the fun of the killing.

I only needed another 15 minutes.

"You are an impressive name to find Bloodheart," I said feeling Genetrix wanting me to leave.

But I couldn't. I could face Bloodheart.

"Do you realise that you are not the only human touched by the Keres Gods?" he asked. "There is another one of you and he is strong, deadly and will kill all life in this galaxy,"

I killed the connection as I felt something stand behind me.

I instantly went for the long magical sword at my waist but I felt a hard knife press against my back.

"Tau'koo," I said hardly impressed that the damn bastard actually had a blade at me.

"There are many within your ranks that do not agree having a human as the leader of the Daughters of Genetrix," Tau'Koo said.

I laughed because he was no Daughter of the Goddess, even I could hear the death, corruption and sickness in his voice. He was not devoted to life, he was the Deathbringer, a servant of Geneitor.

"When did the Father corrupt you?" I asked knowing I could kill him at a moment's notice but I just needed answers.

Immense booms ripped through the air. Huge red flashes raced across the sky.

More missiles rained down on the planet. As did ten thousand little white pods. The ground forces were going to be overwhelmed in moments.

"The Father did not corrupt me. He showed me the truth about the galaxy and how humanity must die, the Keres must die, everyone must die,"

I snapped his neck with a single thought and whipped out my longsword as I went back into the immense library of Life. I was running out of time and I needed my answers.

I went along a narrow marble corridor with thousands of blue leather-bound books lining the shelves. None of them had been touched in decades but the hope of a better life and the magic within the pages kept the dust off them. Hope was a very powerful force in the galaxy.

After a few moments of going along the corridor, I just grinned as I ducked into a small white marble chamber through a small archway. There was a heavy wooden desk in the middle but my translator was dead.

Their body lumped over the damn desk and the ancient text was damaged.

I placed my hands on the translator's forehead, it was still warm and I hated the weird feeling of a warm dead body. It was wrong on so many levels.

"Let me see what never should be seen Mother of Life," I said quietly.

My mind was filled with curiosity, love and happiness as I entered the translator's last final moments. At least they were happy with their last task for the Mother. They were reading a passage about a Soulstone and they were murdered.

I shook my head because it was the Soulstones I was after.

Whoever collected all five shards of Genetrix's being could resurrect her and then she could finally kill her husband once and for all. It was simple and I needed to find all the Soulstones.

I sadly had to push my friend's corpse off the ancient book and their body turned to ash and I clicked my fingers so their soul went to the Mother instead of being tortured by the Father.

There was a bloody fingerprint highlighting one particular section and I couldn't read it. The language made no sense to me because I was a human, not a Keres and I didn't understand long lost languages.

But there was still a little bit of hope.

An immense boom ripped through the library and it sounded like a thousand tons of marble had just come smashing down.

I was seriously running out of time but the preservation of all life in the galaxy was more important than my single life.

I closed my eyes and tried to reconnect with the translator's passing soul but I couldn't. Once a soul was given to Genetrix she kept an iron grip on it.

I just couldn't help but laugh because this was so stupid and I couldn't possibly fail but Bloodheart was coming here. And I had seen in his mind when I connected only moments ago, he knew the ancient language and he knew exactly what I wanted with the Library.

"Return to me Bloodheart," I said as I reconnected with his mind.

I almost jumped as I didn't expect his mind to actually be in the Library. He was here stalking the halls and killing the Keres defenders as he went.

"I was waiting for you," he said, "because I wanted to show you a party trick,"

I screamed in agony as I was pulled through reality and dropped off in front of Bloodheart as him and me were completely alone in the ruined remains of a library.

The white marble walls were smashed and the smoke-veiled sky could easily be seen through the immense holes in the ceiling. There were plenty of Keres corpses littering the ground and I wanted to slaughter him right there and then.

There were even a few smashed marble pillars lining the edges of the library.

Bloodheart in his heavy, thick metal armour pointed his sword at my chest and aimed a pistol at my head.

I went a little cold as I felt my connection with Genetrix fade a little and I just realised that Bloodheart was a son of Geneitor. I had no idea how a human had fallen to the corruption but I was still so new at this.

"You will regret your choice of Patron," Bloodheart said. "The Father kills and he will enjoy you,"

"I regret nothing but why this world? I have been the Daughter of Genetrix for three months now. You have not attacked me in the void, on Ferum or five different worlds. Why this one?"

"Because this world has Keres on it. I love snapping the necks of the Keres as they sleep,"

"You are a monster," I said.

"I am what the galaxy has created me and I will help the Rex rule the stars in Humanity's name. No more Keres, no aliens, no more anything,"

I gasped for a moment as I realised Geneitor didn't have full control over him yet because Bloodheart still wanted humanity to live even though he had said the opposite only moments ago.

Bloodheart still had the weakness and mortality of a human.

He charged.

I thrusted out my hands.

Unleashing torrents of fire.

He flicked a wrist. My torrents went away.

He leapt into the air. Kicking me in the chest.

I fell backwards on the ground.

He landed on me. Kicking me again. Again.

The smell of death, smoke and rotting flesh filled my senses.

I shot out my hands.

Sending him backwards.

I shot up.

I flew at him.

Launching fireball after fireball.

He hissed.

He charged.

I charged.

We raised our swords.

We swung.

Our blades met.

Immense red flashes lit up the sky.

A missile screamed towards us.

I shot out another fireball.

Bloodheart hissed.

The missile smashed down on us.

I slammed my sword into the ground as the missile's explosive power was unleashed, I focused on my love for life, protecting the innocent and hope and a thin shield of dazzling white magical energy formed around me.

Bright flashes of gold, red and orange screamed past me as the deafening roar of an entire building collapsing echoed around me. I had failed the Mother, the Keres and ultimately humanity.

When the collapsing and the fire stopped, I closed my eyes and portalled myself to the top of the ruins where I simply sat on top of the very, very warm marble rubble. I didn't like how it was almost burning my bum but I didn't care because I was thankfully alive.

I hated how the sky was black with immense columns of black smoke veiling the sky. The forest was ablaze and all the little white pods were zooming back up into orbit because they had done their mission and I didn't doubt for a second that Bloodheart was alive.

The only sound of the entire planet now was the constant roaring, crackling and snapping of fires as they devoured all in their path. If there were members of the Dark Keres Cult on the planet then I wouldn't have been surprised if Geneitor was powering the life-destroying flames but thankfully they weren't here.

I just shook my head as I couldn't believe I had completely failed in my mission, then I felt my connection to the Mother restore itself and it felt happy.

A strange joy filled me as I realised that I wasn't just a human now constrained by the limits of a human mind. I was also a Keres with the power of a Goddess behind me, and I started to remember little passages and shards of information from the section of ancient text I had been reading earlier, that was all me.

But I understood it now and I just laughed as I realised my magic must have coursed its way through Bloodheart's mind when we were fighting and it must have found where he kept all his information about the Keres ancient language.

The passage the Translator wanted me to understand was that the Soulstones might have been bought together at one point in history. It was after all the ritual that tried to resurrect Genetrix failing at the same exact time as my own death that brought around my creation.

It was still more than that though, the book was mentioning how the Soulstones never wanted to be apart from each other and they wanted to be found. They would influence the environments, the worlds, the cultures that surrounded them so someone would eventually notice something was seriously wrong in a good or bad way.

I just shook my head because this was basically asking me to understand how the Soulstones had been discovered in the first place and then I could look for similar signs in the present. But the galaxy was a massive place, filled with billions of different planets and a Soulstone could be on any one of them.

I stood up and took a final look at this now-dead world I could sense that a darkness was coming here. Geneitor had a world to consume and he had a lot of dead souls to collect, but I was never going to allow him that for I might be a human but I am Ithane Veilwalker, Daughter of Genetrix and I am a protector of life.

I clicked my fingers and felt my connection with Genetrix strengthen as I collected all the souls on the planets and gifted them to her.

Then I swirled, twirled and whirled my arms about and I opened a bright golden portal to my flagship with my cult. I had a lot of reading to do, a lot of learning and a lot of things to think about because I was making progress and that was a wonderful feeling to have.

One day Genetrix would rise once more and then the entire galaxy would know the meaning of life and death. And only one side would win forever.

AUTHOR OF AGENTS OF THE EMPEROR SERIES

CONNOR WHITELEY

ENFORCEMENT

A SCIENCE FICTION FAR FUTURE SHORT STORY

ENFORCEMENT

This was the day he died and doomed all life in the galaxy forever.

Imperial Ambassador and Enforcer Adrian Shaw took an ugly purple crystal seat at the even darker purple crystal table where he was meant to be meeting one of the damn Keres aliens that humanity had the disservice of ruling over.

He smiled to himself as he sat in the large meeting room if he could actually call it that. Adrian really didn't like how the Keres made everything out of dark purple crystal that flashed, pulsed and hummed ever so slightly. It was a stupid way to design something and it was why he was more than glad humanity ruled over these criminal aliens.

Adrian had fought in the Human-Keres war multiple times, he had even been a General when the Treaty of Defeat was signed and now Adrian was really pleased he got to make sure the evil aliens were following the Treaty to the letter. This was just another calm meeting but Adrian could have sworn that everything just felt a little off.

In case he wasn't just imagining things, like his ex-wife claimed he did every single day, he focused on the perfectly smooth purple crystal walls next to him on both sides and behind him. The walls hardly seemed out of place, they were perfectly smooth, reflective and shiny like they always were.

Adrian couldn't deny that the Keres were evil enough to use

their foul, unnatural magic to try and manipulate him. But he was a human, a God in a galaxy filled with lesser creatures and it was his birthright to rule the stars.

He was simply too smart for the Keres to manipulate him.

Adrian ran his fingers over the perfectly, wonderfully warm crystal table. He really liked how the Keres were clever enough to use their foul magic to make sure everything was body temperature so nothing seemed hot nor cold and everything was good. He was surprised that the Keres were actually intelligent enough to do that.

The sweet aromas of vanilla, strawberries and mint made Adrian smile as the taste of strawberry shortcake formed on his tongue. His mother used to make the most amazing ones, and then Adrian realised he seriously needed to focus in case the foul magic was picking up on his surface thoughts to manipulate him.

It was stupid of the Keres to actually try something that evil so he stood up and went away from the awful chair and crystal and went towards the breathtaking view of the city below.

Adrian had lived in the Keres city for the past five years and it was okay for a stupid alien race. He almost respected the immense purple crystal shards that rose out of the ground and high into the purple sky. Those purple shards were meant to be buildings but Adrian had never wanted to go in one, it simply wasn't natural for something as divine as a human to go into as awful as a Keres building of all things.

He hated these aliens.

Adrian watched the little purple, blue and red crystal discs and pods float through the air as the lazy Keres transported themselves from place to place. He didn't mind them wanting to travel but it was stupid that these mere creatures didn't want to walk.

Having access to good transportation was surely only something creatures as divine as humanity was allowed to have. Adrian really wanted off this awful planet but the Treaty of Defeat had to be maintained no matter the cost and Adrian would do anything to make sure that happened.

Even if it meant annihilating this awful race once and for all.

"Enforcer," a female said behind him.

Adrian took in a deep breath of the vanilla, strawberry and mint scented air and he forced himself to turn around and look at the disgraceful form of the female Keres. The woman was sort of beautiful with her long, thin humanoid features with an unnaturally thin waist, long pretty neck and pointy elf-like features.

He didn't like looking at the awful Keres because it was like they were actually trying to make a mockery of the divinity of humanity. This woman was just as disgraceful as all the other versions of her kin.

"It is an honour to see you again," the woman said. "I can assure the Imperium and the Glorious Rex himself that Keres are living in ways conducive to the Treaty of Defeat,"

Adrian shook his head and took out a data slate. "That is a lie and you know it, Keres scum. The Treaty of Defeat Section 5c and 9a make it illegal for the Keres to have a form of social activity,"

"We do not have social activities," the woman said like Adrian was an idiot.

"Humans are the only people that are allowed social activity and they are gambling, smoking and clubbing," Adrian said. "The Keres are not allowed,"

"And I have yet to see any evidence of this so-called activities," the woman said and Adrian realised that she was now floating up in the air.

"Our spies took these photos of the Keres doing some kind of singing, dancing and partying," Adrian said passing the woman the photos.

Adrian hated to look at them because they were clearly dangerous, evil and beyond contempt to the righteousness of humanity. All the Keres in the photos were singing and dancing around some kind of corpse and it was just disgusting to look at.

The woman clicked her fingers and the air crackled. Adrian really wished he had bought a gun with him and a massive one at that.

"This isn't an example of social activity. These were taken two weeks ago I presume during the Feast of Life,"

Adrian rolled his eyes. He had no idea why humanity didn't just nuke this pointless alien race in the first place, especially with them continuing to bang on about their damn mythology.

He was aware of how the so-called Feast of Life was meant to honour the even more so-called Goddess of Life Genetrix. The woman that had apparently created humanity and Keres from different arms of hers.

"It is just stupid you continue to believe in lies," Adrian said hating this woman, "if you would simply abandon those ways then the Rex might treat you better,"

The woman grinned at him. "Enforcer, the problem with humanity is that you continue to ignore basic facts about the galaxy. In fact it is amazing you humans even manage to grasp the grandeur of the universe,"

Adrian really wished he had a gun about now. How dare this woman challenge the righteousness of humanity.

"All of us know that Genetrix and the God of Death Geneitor are alive and well. And their total rebirth can only happen when someone collects the Soul Stones of their God Children,"

Adrian laughed. Now she was being beyond stupid. The entire idea of Gods, Goddesses and their so-called divine children was just an insult.

As much as Adrian wanted to condemn this race for lunacy he sadly had other business to question.

"And there have been ten attacks on Imperial warships by Keres elements in the past year. That is a clear violation of the Treaty,"

"Yet humanity continues to massacre my people," the Keres woman said. "Tell me enforcer how many millions of my people have been murdered by humans in the past year,"

Adrian stood up and paced around the disgusting office for a moment. He didn't doubt that she was well aware of the disgraceful attacks against innocent humans and if this was part of a massive

Keres revenge plot then he had to find out what was happening.

He even considered he might have to be nice to her, a Keres of all things, to make sure she gave him the information.

"I don't know but I don't support murder of any kind," Adrian said as he felt a pressure building against his mind.

"You lie," the woman said. "You seek information human. I can see your thoughts as clear as day and you want to wipe out my race,"

Adrian fell to his knees as the pressure built and built.

"I can see your fear human," the woman said. "You might deny the existence of Genetrix but she gives me power and she sees your soul. You have murdered thousands in the name of your false divinity and now… you have attracted the sight of Geneitor,"

Adrian forced himself up despite the agony that was pouring out of his knees.

"That makes sense. Geneitor would want to corrupt young, stupid minds like humanity to serve him and actually I can show you the true grandeur of the galaxy if you want me to,"

Adrian instantly realised that this was no one from the normal Keres. This woman or whatever foul creature she had to be from one of the extremist factions that wanted to save the stupid Keres races.

Adrian reached for a gun that wasn't there and the woman laughed.

"Now meet your true God or learn the truth about the Keres. Tell us see what Fate Geneitor has chosen for you,"

Adrian screamed as he felt the world fall away from him.

***

He had no idea how long he was out for but Adrian was guessing maybe an hour or two. He found himself standing in the middle of some strange black sandy desert with a pitch black sky that he didn't recognise. He knew this couldn't be something in the known galaxy because it just didn't feel like it.

The entire area was icy cold and the awful wind that rushed past him reminded Adrian of being in a wind tunnel back at university, but the weird thing was that his hair wasn't moving. He could hear and see the wind. He couldn't feel it.

He tried to strain his eyes in an effort to see if anything was out here. Maybe there was a structure, maybe a fellow human or maybe there was something else anything.

It was way too dark for that and Adrian felt completely alone for the first time ever. At least he was a divine human and he was a God amongst all the other creatures in the galaxy so he would be fine.

Then the wind just stopped and it looked like there was a person on fire in the distance.

Adrian went over to the person. As soon as Adrian saw the poor innocent human on the ground he felt sorry for the man. His flesh was charred, smouldering and deeply damaged.

But the deep dark deep sapphire eyes were okay and they just focused on him.

"Are you the one I sent myself in the future?" the man asked.

Adrian had no idea but it was clear the evil Keres had done this to the poor, innocent human. This was why they had to die and be wiped out.

"I can sense your hate, your ignorance and your humanity," the man said. "Yes, you are the man I sent from the future. Interesting I thought humans would be a little taller,"

"What are you?" Adrian asked wanting to return to Earth immediately to ask the Rex to annihilate the Keres forever.

"I am Geneitor," the man said, "or what is left of him. I am sorry but if I survived in the future then it means I kill you in a few moments. Don't be scared. It isn't that painful, just a little learning process first of all,"

Adrian went to run away but he screamed in agony as he felt the man chomp into his legs. Shattering bones and ripping out chunks of his flesh.

"Tasty," Geneitor said. "Do you have a question whilst I finish off your leg?"

Adrian watched in utter horror as Geneitor held his left leg like a chicken drumstick and sucked the blood before chomping on it.

"What the hell is this place?"

"A good question," Geneitor said licking some blood off his hand. "This is about 4 billion years ago. Earth has only just about formed and this is the Aftermath of the War of Divinity,"

Adrian shrugged.

"This is where me and my wife had a war to end all wars, you humans might say. She was all about life and creating it and I was fucked off with her. So I want to kill everything she ever created,"

Adrian shook his head. It was a shame that Geneitor hadn't won the war at least that way the Keres would be dead.

"My wife created the Keres and humans to survive side by side but that wasn't enough for me. I corrupted humanity and made them win for me against my wife and the Keres,"

"Good," Adrian said.

Genitor wiped his mouth again. "Humans are just as stupid now as before because all you people do is hate. You hate the Keres out of fear but actually, they are the creatures keeping you alive,"

"How?" Adrian asked looking away as Geneitor took another chomp on his leg.

"Simple. In the future when I am recovered and when the Keres uncover my relics that will corrupt them. I will start to return to my consciousness then I will whisper lies into the ears of some Keres but a lot of humans about why the Keres have to die,"

"The Human-Keres war? That was all you,"

"That is brilliant to know. At least I know my relics are found and I am successful," Geneitor said. "I'll have to give you a quick death for that alone,"

Adrian shook his head. Damn this alien God.

"Then I will continue to corrupt the Keres and humanity, and of course my wife will have plans laid too. But she was a lot more injured than I was so I will return first and then my job will simply be to hunt down and kill whatever Cult springs up to resurrect Genetrix,"

"What happens if you fail?" Adrian asked.

Geneitor laughed as his crackling, charred body stood up and looked at Adrian like he was a tasty piece of meat.

"I will not fail. Genetrix will not be resurrected and then finally the Keres, my wife and humanity will all die. Then I will move onto another galaxy and then I will repeat everything again. All life must die and you must die so I can escape into Ultraspace and sleep until my Cult finds me,"

"No," Adrian said as Geneitor unleashed his death magic on him.

And as he died Adrian could only focus on the sheer stupidity of humanity because it wasn't the Keres manipulating humanity, it was a God they didn't believe in.

It was even worse that Adrian couldn't tell anyone because he would die billions of years into a past humanity didn't even know existed because the Rex had outlawed history. Something else he guessed Geneitor had made him do.

And something Adrian was going to regret enforcing forever.

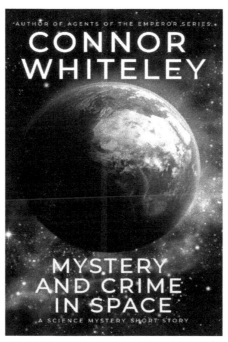

GET YOUR FREE SHORT STORY NOW! And get signed up to Connor Whiteley's newsletter to hear about new gripping books, offers and exciting projects. (You'll never be sent spam)

https://www.subscribepage.io/garrosignup

About the author:

Connor Whiteley is the author of over 60 books in the sci-fi fantasy, nonfiction psychology and books for writer's genre and he is a Human Branding Speaker and Consultant.

He is a passionate warhammer 40,000 reader, psychology student and author.

Who narrates his own audiobooks and he hosts The Psychology World Podcast.

All whilst studying Psychology at the University of Kent, England.

Also, he was a former Explorer Scout where he gave a speech to the Maltese President in August 2018 and he attended Prince Charles' 70th Birthday Party at Buckingham Palace in May 2018.

Plus, he is a self-confessed coffee lover!

Other books by Connor Whiteley:
Bettie English Private Eye Series
A Very Private Woman
The Russian Case
A Very Urgent Matter
A Case Most Personal
Trains, Scots and Private Eyes
The Federation Protects
Cops, Robbers and Private Eyes
Just Ask Bettie English
An Inheritance To Die For
The Death of Graham Adams
Bearing Witness
The Twelve
The Wrong Body
The Assassination Of Bettie English
Wining And Dying
Eight Hours
Uniformed Cabal
A Case Most Christmas

Gay Romance Novellas
Breaking, Nursing, Repairing A Broken Heart
Jacob And Daniel
Fallen For A Lie
Spying And Weddings
Clean Break
Awakening Love
Meeting A Country Man
Loving Prime Minister
Snowed In Love
Never Been Kissed

Love Betrays You
Love And Hurt

Lord of War Origin Trilogy:
Not Scared Of The Dark
Madness
Burn Them All

Way Of The Odyssey
Odyssey of Rebirth
Convergence of Odysseys
Odyssey Of Hope
Odyssey of Enlightment

Lady Tano Fantasy Adventure Stories
Betrayal
Murder
Annihilation

Agents of The Emperor
Deceitful Terra
Blood And Wrath
Infiltration
Fuel To The Fire
Return of The Ancient Ones
Vigilance
Angels of Fire
Kingmaker
The Eight
The Lost Generation
Hunt
Emperor's Council

Speaker of Treachery
Birth Of The Empire
Terraforma
Spaceguard

The Rising Augusta Fantasy Adventure Series
Rise To Power
Rising Walls
Rising Force
Rising Realm

The Fireheart Fantasy Series
Heart of Fire
Heart of Lies
Heart of Prophecy
Heart of Bones
Heart of Fate

City of Assassins (Urban Fantasy)
City of Death
City of Martyrs
City of Pleasure
City of Power

Lord Of War Trilogy (Agents of The Emperor)
Not Scared Of The Dark
Madness
Burn It All Down

Miscellaneous:
Dead Names
RETURN
FREEDOM
SALVATION
Reflection of Mount Flame
The Masked One
The Great Deer
English Independence

OTHER SHORT STORIES BY CONNOR WHITELEY
Mystery Short Story Collections
Criminally Good Stories Volume 1: 20 Detective Mystery Short Stories
Criminally Good Stories Volume 2: 20 Private Investigator Short Stories
Criminally Good Stories Volume 3: 20 Crime Fiction Short Stories
Criminally Good Stories Volume 4: 20 Science Fiction and Fantasy Mystery Short Stories
Criminally Good Stories Volume 5: 20 Romantic Suspense Short Stories

Connor Whiteley Starter Collections:
Agents of The Emperor Starter Collection
Bettie English Starter Collection
Matilda Plum Starter Collection
Gay Romance Starter Collection
Way Of The Odyssey Starter Collection
Kendra Detective Fiction Starter Collection

Science Fiction Short Story Collections
Rivetingly Great Stories Volume 1
Rivetingly Great Stories Volume 2
Rivetingly Great Stories Volume 3
Rivetingly Great Stories Volume 4
Rivetingly Great Stories Volume 5

Mystery Short Stories:
Protecting The Woman She Hated
Finding A Royal Friend
Our Woman In Paris
Corrupt Driving
A Prime Assassination
Jubilee Thief
Jubilee, Terror, Celebrations
Negative Jubilation
Ghostly Jubilation
Killing For Womenkind
A Snowy Death
Miracle Of Death
A Spy In Rome
The 12:30 To St Pancreas
A Country In Trouble
A Smokey Way To Go
A Spicy Way To GO
A Marketing Way To Go
A Missing Way To Go
A Showering Way To Go
Poison In The Candy Cane
Kendra Detective Mystery Collection Volume 1
Kendra Detective Mystery Collection Volume 2
Mystery Short Story Collection Volume 1

Mystery Short Story Collection Volume 2
Criminal Performance
Candy Detectives
Key To Birth In The Past

Science Fiction Short Stories:
Their Brave New World
Gummy Bear Detective
The Candy Detective
What Candies Fear
The Blurred Image
Shattered Legions
The First Rememberer
Life of A Rememberer
System of Wonder
Lifesaver
Remarkable Way She Died
The Interrogation of Annabella Stormic

Fantasy Short Stories:
City of Snow
City of Light
City of Vengeance
Dragons, Goats and Kingdom
Smog The Pathetic Dragon
Don't Go In The Shed
The Tomato Saver
The Remarkable Way She Died
Dragon Coins
Dragon Tea
Dragon Rider

All books in 'An Introductory Series':
Introduction To Psychotherapies
I Am Not A Victim, I Am A Survivor
Breaking The Silence
Healing As A Survivor
Clinical Psychology and Transgender Clients
Clinical Psychology
Moral Psychology
Myths About Clinical Psychology
401 Statistics Questions For Psychology Students
Careers In Psychology
Psychology of Suicide
Dementia Psychology
Clinical Psychology Reflections Volume 4
Forensic Psychology of Terrorism And Hostage-Taking
Forensic Psychology of False Allegations
Year In Psychology
CBT For Anxiety
CBT For Depression
Applied Psychology
BIOLOGICAL PSYCHOLOGY 3RD EDITION
COGNITIVE PSYCHOLOGY THIRD EDITION
SOCIAL PSYCHOLOGY- 3RD EDITION
ABNORMAL PSYCHOLOGY 3RD EDITION
PSYCHOLOGY OF RELATIONSHIPS- 3RD EDITION
DEVELOPMENTAL PSYCHOLOGY 3RD EDITION
HEALTH PSYCHOLOGY
RESEARCH IN PSYCHOLOGY
A GUIDE TO MENTAL HEALTH AND TREATMENT
AROUND THE WORLD- A GLOBAL LOOK AT
DEPRESSION
FORENSIC PSYCHOLOGY